After Pa Was Shot

After Pa Was Shot

Judy Alter

MAGGIE  BOOKS

Ellen C. Temple Publishing and E-Heart Press

Copyright © 1991 Alter Children's Trust

Library of Congress Cataloging-in-Publication Data
Alter, Judy, 1938-
  After Pa was shot/Judy Alter.
    p. cm.
  Summary: A thirteen-year-old girl's life in turn-of-the-century
Texas is drastically altered when her father is killed.
  ISBN 0-936650-12-5
  [1. Death—Fiction. 2. Texas—Fiction.] I. Title.
PZ7.A4636Af 1990   89-12176
[Fic]—dc20   CIP
                                                          AC

This edition is a reprint of the original published
by William Morrow and Co. in 1978.
Printed in the United States of America
Reproduction or use of this book in whole or in part in any manner
without written permission of the publisher is strictly prohibited.

Published jointly by:

Ellen C. Temple Publishing Inc.   E-Heart Press Inc.
      5030 Champions Drive   3700 Mockingbird Lane
        Lufkin, TX 75901   Dallas, TX 75205

Printed on acid-free, 60 percent recycled paper.

Cover art and drawing by Charles Shaw
Production by Dodson Publication Services, Austin, Texas

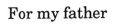

For my father

After Pa Was Shot

1

Pa was shot the day after Christmas the year I was twelve. It was one of those balmy December days that fool you into thinking there won't be a winter that year, and Bobby Joe, my little brother, had begged and pleaded until we played his favorite game, cowboys and Indians. Both of us were perched in the old live-oak tree in front of our house, scanning the horizon for redskins. We didn't see any, of course, but we did see Uncle Charlie running down the road, as if he'd lost all his sense.

"Your pa's been shot!" he shouted at us, which sounded so crazy that we stared in disbelief. Uncle Charlie was Pa's younger brother and a great cutup, always playing jokes on everyone, even Ma, so we never did believe half of what he said. This time we didn't believe him at all.

"See any Indians?" B.J. asked me, ignoring Uncle Charlie and his announcement.

But I didn't answer. I sat there and watched Uncle Charlie take the rickety front steps two at a time, and it struck me that he was telling the truth and he was in a hurry to break the news to Ma before the whole town arrived at our gate. And then I heard a lot of noise off in the distance. Down the road to town a disorganized parade appeared headed our way, and I looked long and hard before I realized that the object in the center was my father. Someone had fashioned a kind of stretcher and four men carried it, while others ran around the edges. Everyone was telling everyone else what to do, but over the whole clatter I heard a voice calling, "Get the doc! Get the doc!"

"Come on, B.J., quick!" I nearly pushed him out of the tree in my haste to be hidden before they all got to our house. As we scrambled down, I heard one loud piercing scream from Ma, and I put my hands over my ears to blot out the sound and all it meant.

B.J. was still kind of dazed and followed me blindly as I pulled him around the corner of the house where we could peek in a window to the living room and still be hidden behind a bare but thick honeysuckle vine so the men wouldn't spot us when they brought Pa in. I think I really wanted to hide us so we wouldn't have to see Pa.

We did peek in the window and saw Ma sitting in a rocking chair, straight as a stick, her hands thrown out and her eyes staring straight ahead. She looked as though she had frozen in the position she took when Uncle Charlie blurted out the news. Uncle Charlie, having unburdened himself of his announcement, was walking up and down, awkwardly holding Little Henry, the baby of our family, and murmuring, "Now, Lucille," in a kind of desperate tone. Later I found out that when he told Ma about the shooting, without preparing her at all, just bringing it right out, Ma nearly dropped the baby. Uncle Charlie was there to catch him, but Uncle Charlie wasn't much with babies, and he looked as if he would drop Little Henry himself any minute.

The parade with Pa had reached our front gate by now, and Doc Mason had made it to the head of the line. "Bring him on in," he ordered, "but be careful." Doc shoved the gate harder than its rusted hinges were meant to take, and it sagged and stuck open just a crack. He gave it a good kick and sent it flying out of the way of the men who carried Pa.

"Ellsbeth?"

"What, B.J.?"

"Is Pa dead?"

"Don't know. But I don't think so, not the way Doc Mason was carrying on."

"You gonna go in and find out?"

"No." That may sound silly. My pa was in there, and I didn't know if he was alive or dead, but I didn't want to know. At twelve years old, you know by instinct what you later learn by bitter lesson—bad news doesn't exist until you hear it. If I went in the house, I might find out that Pa was really dead and I wouldn't have a hope to cling to, so I stayed outside where I could clutch at the possibility the bullet had barely grazed him.

If I had been thinking about Ma, I would have gone in to take care of the baby, but then there were enough people in there. Someone would watch after Little Henry. And I wasn't thinking about Ma. I was thinking about Pa . . . and me.

I just started walking away from the house, and B.J. followed me, both of us silent for a long time. The old house we lived in was on the far edge of town, with fields and stands of loblolly pines behind it, and one big tank where some ducks swam. In summer, when Pa let us, we swam in it too, even though Ma said we'd catch our death of something in that dirty water. For some reason I just headed for that pond, with B.J. trailing along.

"Ellsbeth?"

"What now, B.J.?"

"You suppose Pa was shot defending the bank from robbers?"

"You been listening to the old men talk too much, B.J. There aren't any gangs like the James brothers anymore." Because our last name was James too, B.J. was always fascinated by the famous outlaws and turned them into heroes.

"Well, somebody could have robbed the bank. I bet my pa was a hero!"

"Of course he was a hero!" I answered fiercely. I wanted to explain that it didn't matter how Pa got shot, but I didn't. B.J. needed to believe in the Wild West and to put Pa's shooting into that setting, and I tried to be gentle with him.

"B.J., this is Center, Texas, in 1904. There aren't any more bank-robbery gangs and shootings in the street and all that. You just hear people talk about it, and you see those posters advertising the Wild West shows. But that can't be how Pa got shot. We'll just have to find out when we go home."

"You ready to go back to the house?"

"No." We had reached the edge of the stock tank,

and I stood there looking into the depths of its dirty water, so murky that it didn't even reflect the pines that bordered the far edge. Idly, I reached down and picked up a rock, then another, and began chunking rocks, watching the waves ripple out and thinking about Pa. Pa wasn't only my pa; he was almost the best friend I had. He understood about long, skinny girls who wished they could wear pants instead of dresses and who chunked rocks like boys and had no interest in sewing a fine seam. Ma couldn't fathom it, herself a seamstress, and she kept trying to get me to learn to sew. And to play the piano. That was another sore point. My fingers were clumsy, not meant for fine work or precise notes, and my soul was impatient with practice. Only Pa understood and said, "Leave the girl be, Lucille."

The old gander started toward us, scolding, and B.J. chunked a rock at him instead of into the water. It was enough to break my reverie, and I jumped on him.

"You know Pa doesn't let us throw rocks at the ducks or anything—even that mean old gander!"

"It was gonna chase me," he whined.

"Come on, I reckon it's time to go back."

"Okay."

Reluctantly I headed toward the house. B.J. hurried out of impatience, but I lingered from dread.

Slowly the house in the distance grew closer, and soon I could even make out the faces of a group of men standing in the yard, hands in their pockets. They looked down at the ground and only occasionally glanced at each other, mostly watching their own feet, which idly kicked at the clay and pebbles on the ground. Long before I could hear their voices, I heard our chickens, scolding these intruders in their domain. Someone had tied Buck, the stallion that was Pa's pride and joy and Ma's terror, to a sturdy part of the fence in the far corner of the yard, and he snorted nervously from time to time. Most people, even in Center, had grass in front of their houses. We had clay and a horse and chickens, and once in a while one of the chickens landed on our dinner table, but never before it was old and stringy.

I reached out and grabbed B.J.'s hand to slow him down so we could watch for a minute. A horse and cart pulled up by the now-broken gate, and a stern, spare woman got out.

"Aunt Nelda!" B.J. whispered in disgust.

"Yeah. Darn."

Ma's sister had arrived, brought by Uncle Fred, whose fate it had been to marry that domineering and determined woman. Some people said it was his good luck, but I clung to a belief that it was his misfortune. Aunt Nelda was one of the world's bosses, without a stitch of humor in her makeup or any appreciation for the speculative side of life. And she sure was a mismatch for Uncle Fred, who always had a scheme to get rich. These days he wanted to join the other farmers who were leaving their fields to search for oil. Ever since the gusher had come in down to Beaumont a few years before, oil was on everybody's mind.

"Look at what's happening down around Beaumont," Uncle Fred would say. "Those people are making money hand over fist. Why I might even find oil right here around Center. It's all over East Texas, you know, and all you got to do is get you a wiggle stick and go looking on some creek." Sometimes he would ask Pa to go, and Pa would laugh and say sure, he'd go one day. We kids thought it sounded exciting, and we hung on every word about creekology and wildcatters and the fortune that covered East Texas in black gold.

But Aunt Nelda would have none of it. "You'll do no such thing, Fred Dawson! We're farmers, always have been, and proud of it. You won't mess with that stuff and all the riffraff that's looking for a pot at the end of the rainbow."

And Uncle Fred would subside and forget about oil for a while. Pa always looked sort of sad after that, as if he was sorry for Uncle Fred.

And now Aunt Nelda had come to take charge of

our house in the hour of our need. I knew that's what relatives did, come when needed, but oh, how I resented her!

Uncle Fred hitched the horse to what was left of the front fence and joined the men in the yard. We inched by them to go in the house, and they eyed us solemnly, nodding their heads just a bit in greeting. We stared back, not knowing what to do or say. As we mounted the steps, B.J.'s impatience left him and he caught my reluctance. In fact, I near had to pull him through the door.

Aunt Nelda opened the door just as I reached for it and looked right over us. "Fred, come in here and help heat some water," she demanded. Then she spied us. "Where have you children been? Your ma needs you. Get in here right now."

We obeyed. Ma didn't really need us. She was sitting in the same rocking chair, still staring straight ahead, not aware of who was around her. Doc Mason stood in front of her, kind of biting his lip and looking at a worn spot in the rug. I had an impulse to run to Ma and just hug her or something, but I felt as if I should say something too, and I didn't know what, so I just looked at her and didn't say anything. She didn't even see me.

Doc was talking to her. "I can't hold out much hope, Lucille. Parker's been shot bad through the vital organs, and I can't do much for him. Just feed him broth, keep the wound clean, and pray. But I don't have much faith. You'd best prepare yourself for the worst."

"Doc"—Aunt Nelda jumped into the silence left by Ma's inability to talk—"is he conscious?"

"Oh, yeah, sure. And in pretty good spirits, too, considering. He knows what the situation is. Asked and I told him outright."

My pa was alive! My heart did flip-flops, and I wanted to jump in the air, but I just squeezed B.J.'s hand, and he grinned at me. We didn't care how much faith Doc had, we knew there was hope and we clung to it. It was a lot more comforting at that moment to be a child and believe than to know, as Doc and Ma did, what was going to happen.

Aunt Nelda spotted us again, and the mere fact that we were standing still, doing nothing, galled her. She set out to correct the situation at once. "Ellsbeth! You take Little Henry. He's underfoot and your ma can't handle him right now. Bobby Joe, you go outside and help Brother Anderson. He's getting wood for the stove."

I didn't even know the minister was at the house, let alone out in the backyard gathering wood, and I smothered a grin at the idea that Aunt Nelda had the nerve to put him to work the minute she got in the house. Shoving B.J. toward the kitchen to help the poor man, I went to take Little Henry, who was upset by all the confusion and people. He was almost a year old and learning to cry out "Ma, Ma," which he now managed to scream between sobs. I got the wagon we kept in the house and seated him on the pillow in it and began to pull him through the house. This was our standard method for quieting Little Henry, and it usually worked, but not this time. I kept pulling, and he kept screaming.

"Now stay out of people's way with that wagon, Ellsbeth!"

"Yes, ma'am." There wasn't any use getting mad at her, I supposed. She was only trying to do what she thought was helpful, and it was just her way that was unfortunate.

One by one, people were going in to see Pa. "Don't tire him out," Doc would warn, but he let them see him. It took some convincing for Ma to go. She wanted to, of course, but she was afraid of what she'd find, afraid she'd break down and cry, and just generally afraid. I guess she felt the way I did when I went to the tank to chunk rocks instead of coming into the house. What you don't know can't hurt you.

Uncle Charlie went with Ma, and they stayed only a few minutes, then came out with Uncle Charlie holding Ma, who was covering her face with her hands. I felt sorry for Uncle Charlie. He was Pa's only brother, and they were good friends, and he was bound to be more upset than almost anybody, except maybe Ma. Besides, for all his jokes and tricks, Uncle Charlie was a good and kind man.

Brother Anderson went in and stayed longer, praying I suppose, and even Aunt Nelda took a turn, though I couldn't imagine that Pa would want to see her. Nobody thought to ask if I wanted to see Pa, but I did, desperately. I waited until it seemed everyone had their chance, and Doc had announced that it was time for Pa to rest. Little Henry had finally stopped screaming and fallen into an exhausted sleep, so I parked his wagon in a corner and snuck to the door of the bedroom.

I checked all around before opening the door to make sure no one would see me, but they were all busy, mostly with their own grieving. Ma was still crying, and Brother Anderson was trying to comfort her. Aunt Nelda was busy in the kitchen, and Uncle Charlie stood staring out the window, lost in thought and looking so alone that if I hadn't been bent on going in to see Pa, I would have gone over and held his hand. I had no idea where B.J. had gotten to, but I suspected he was hiding from Aunt Nelda.

Nobody was looking at me. I opened the door just a crack and slipped into the bedroom. Pa was propped partway up with pillows, lying there with his eyes closed, but he didn't look any different from usual. I tiptoed to the bed and stood there, silent as a mouse. It was a long time before he turned his head, opened his eyes, and saw me.

"Hi, Lollipop." He grinned at me, and I knew everything was all right if my pa could grin and call me by his pet nickname for me. I had a fondness for lollipops that exceeded even the normal liking of most children, and Pa had long before taken to calling me "Lollipop."

"Hi, Pa." It didn't seem to me I should ask him how he was, so I just stood there, waiting.

"I'm glad you came to see me, Lollipop. I need to talk to you. Did you hear what Doc said about me?"

"That he expected the worst?" How could I say, in words, that he might die? "Yeah, I heard, but I know he's wrong."

"No, Lollipop, he's not wrong," Pa said gently. "It's true, and it's something we all have to face. And I have to talk to you particularly, because you're the oldest and the one who can help your ma the most with the other children and the house."

"But I don't have to play the piano?"

He grinned, such a nice grin to see. "No, but you will have to help your ma. I expect she's going to have a hard time. She's used to being taken care of,

21

and now she'll be the head of the family. You'll have to help with the little ones. Did you know Ma's going to have another baby?"

My eyes flew wide open. "Really?"

This time Pa looked really sad, and his voice was resigned when he said, "Yes. That means there'll be four of you children for her to look after, and one of them a brand-new baby before Henry is even old enough to take care of himself. I'm worried about your ma."

"I'll help her, Pa, I really will."

"I know you will."

I had the feeling Pa was trying to tell me good-bye and be good, but he couldn't quite bring himself to say so, and I sure didn't want to hear those words. Even if Pa really was going to leave us, I didn't want to face it. After a minute Pa changed the subject.

"Want to see where I got shot?"

"Yeah, Pa, if you want to show me."

And he showed me where the bullet went into him, low on the right side, and told me that it went up through his liver and stopped somewhere in his back. Doc didn't have any way of getting it out, which was the problem. I didn't know much about anatomy or medicine or any of that, but I knew the liver was important. When people talked about someone who was "sick in the liver," he was always in a bad way. So I knew Pa's condition was serious if his liver was involved.

I didn't really like looking at that hole in his side, but he had wanted me to and I did. Then he pulled the covers up around him and reached out for my hand. I stood there a long time, holding his hand tight, neither of us saying anything, until finally he said, "Lollipop, I think you better go on. I need to sleep, and Aunt Nelda will be looking for you."

"Yes, Pa. I'll be back later." But I didn't want to leave the room.

2

Pa was shot because he was acting sheriff over the Christmas holiday. He had been elected to a regular term as deputy sheriff, but his time was up just before Christmas. He and Ma had words about it.

"Parker, I don't want you to serve another term as deputy sheriff."

"Lucille," Pa answered patiently, "you know it gives us a little extra money, and Lord knows we need that."

I was eavesdropping outside the kitchen the night

24

this conversation went on, but I could just imagine the look on Ma's face when she answered him.

"We can get along on what you make from Wilkerson's Dry-Goods Store . . . and I'll take in sewing again."

"You'll do no such thing," Pa stormed, having lost his patience rather quickly. "You raise the children, and I'll support the family." Then his voice softened to the tone he often used to gentle Ma to his point of view. "Besides, you know I like being deputy sheriff. It gives me a chance to walk around town and visit with everybody after being stuck behind a counter all day long."

"Please, for the children and me." Ma could sound very appealing when she wanted!

"Damn and blast!" Pa could get angry, too. "It's partly for the children and you I do it. It's for the children and you that I'm stuck in a dry-goods store, moldering before I'm forty, when I should be out West raising cattle on my own land and working for myself."

Ma ignored that comment. It was an old argument between them. Pa wanted desperately to be a rancher, to raise his family on his own land in the outdoors, and he once went so far as to put money down on some land way out in West Texas, but Ma was afraid to go. Center was close to relatives, his and hers, and she said it was a "civilized" place to raise her children. Now, instead of reopening that bag of troubles, she retreated to the subject of deputy sheriff.

"Someday," she predicted ominously, "something could happen to you."

"Nonsense. The most I ever do is put a drunk in jail or go after someone who's behind in his debts. There's no danger, Lucille. This is Center, Texas, 1904, not Dodge City, Kansas, in 1890."

It was true not much went on in Center. I guess there must have been five hundred people then, and we knew most of them. Our town was one of those stopping places for a lot of Southerners, both black and white, when they fled the South during the Civil War. Some stopped for a while and then moved on; others stayed. Ma's parents had stayed, and none of the Clemson line ever got over believing they had been rich gentry back in Alabama. Now they clung together in this town of Center, and not one of them could be moved.

Not that Center was very much. By 1904 we had board sidewalks, a schoolhouse, three churches, the dry-goods store where Pa worked, a railroad station, and an opera house. Civilization had settled over East Texas long ago, and the Wild West existed only in the dreams of kids like B.J. Nobody ever robbed the bank or shot anybody or even stole a horse—though old Mrs. Hobb's milk cow disappeared once—and it was true all Pa did was go after drunks and people who didn't pay their bills. But B.J. and I were awful proud that our pa was a deputy sheriff, and we stood inches taller every time he buckled on that .44 to go out and make the rounds in town. As I listened by the kitchen door that night, I prayed that Pa would win the argument because I wanted him to go on being deputy sheriff.

"Remember," Ma began again, "the night you brought a desperate criminal to this house, this very house where your children and wife slept thinking they were safe?"

"Desperate criminal? You mean poor old Jenkins, who couldn't pay his bills? He wouldn't hurt a flea, and probably the hardest thing I ever had to do as sheriff was tell that old man I had to arrest him because he owed too much to James Wilkerson at the store."

I remembered the night. It was winter and a norther had blown through, leaving bitter cold behind. Pa had to go way out in the country to arrest Jenkins and bring him in. We never did know that man's full name. All we knew was Jenkins and that he had a son who had gone to the oil fields the first he heard about the boom. But the son got kicked off the crew, the way all the blacks did in those days, and he had disappeared. Jenkins seemed to lose his heart after that and never did anything, including paying his bills.

Anyway, Pa went after him this cold night, but there wasn't any fire lit in the jail and it was stone cold, so Pa brought the old man to our house. He took a bunch of blankets to make a pallet for him on the floor on the back porch, which wasn't exactly warm, but it was better than the jail. Pitiful as Jenkins was, Pa took the precaution to chain him to the old cot we kept out there, and then Pa himself slept on the cot. Of course, we didn't know this until we waked up next morning, but Ma raised holy Ned with Pa because she thought he had put us all in danger. He promised never to do that again. I don't think Ma would have objected so much if Jenkins hadn't been a man of color.

Pa and Ma really loved each other, but they looked at life differently. Pa saw all the joy, and Ma always expected the worst. Usually she found it, and usually Pa was involved. But I will have to say I never heard her say "I told you so." Never, and there were a lot of times she could have said it. But Pa always won her over. He would turn repentant, promise never to do it again, whether it was chain a prisoner to the cot or take us swimming in the tank, and then he'd wrap his arms around Ma. She always forgave him.

That was just what happened about being deputy sheriff that night in December. Much as it meant to Pa, he gave it up for Ma and promised her he would never wear that .44 again. I tiptoed back to bed in dejection, tempted to wake B.J. and tell him the bad news, but then I guessed it would keep until morning.

However, fate stepped in, and Pa served one more spell as deputy. The real sheriff, Luke Green, had a sick mother who lived in a town about forty miles away. She wasn't expected to live long, and Sheriff Green wanted to spend Christmas with her, so he asked Pa to take over while he was gone. He promised to come back on the morning train the day after Christmas.

"Lucille, what could I do?" Pa asked. "The man's mother is dying."

"You're right, Parker, it was the only thing to do. But tell him it's the last time."

"I promise."

That Christmas morning we opened our gifts together. B.J. got a cowboy hat and a pair of boots and a fake tin star that looked like a real sheriff's badge. I ached with envy of him when I opened my presents—a ruffled apron and a set of tea dishes. Ma was always trying to make a lady of me, and I wanted to be a sheriff, even a pretend one like B.J. But Pa had saved back one present for me, and he gave it to me at the last of our Christmas morning celebration. It was a leather bridle for Buck.

"There, Lollipop. You can replace that old piece of rope you use."

I could hardly wait to rush out and put the bridle on Buck, but I was supposed to help with Christmas dinner and Ma frowned so hard that I postponed my first ride. As it happened, I never did get to use that bridle, but at the time I was overcome with pure joy.

After dinner, Pa left for town since he was the officer on duty. He came in late at night and went out again once or twice during the night. But he never let on the next morning that anything had happened, and we didn't know anything was wrong until Uncle Charlie had come running up.

After I talked to Pa and saw where the bullet had hit him, I guess I knew it was bad. I just tried not to think about it.

Doc Mason left, saying Pa was resting as comfortably as he could, and he'd come back in the evening to check on him. Aunt Nelda had put Ma to bed with a cold rag on her head, and Little Henry was still sleeping, so I didn't have any responsibilities. I wandered outside, where there was still a knot of men kicking at the ground and disturbing our chickens.

As I edged past the men, I heard one say, "No,

that's not what happened at all. Let me tell you the way I know it." I inched closer and stood as silent and unobtrusive as I could.

"Seems like Parker was just checking things out on Christmas day when somebody came to him and says that Ben Short was making an awful row in the middle of town. Been drinking too much and was hollering. Not all of it nice language neither." The speaker chuckled a little. "And Parker, of course, thought it was his duty to tell Short to go on home and quit making such a fuss. He talked to him, but it just made Short madder. You know what liquor can do to people."

A lot of pious nods confirmed the evil effects of liquor, and the storyteller went on, with me hanging on every word.

"Parker went back around town about an hour later, and Short was still there, shouting and carrying on. So this time Parker warned him that if he didn't get off the streets peaceable, he'd have to put him in jail. I was there. I heard this part. Short says, 'I dare you,' and Parker warns him, 'Don't push me, Ben. Go on home and enjoy Christmas with your family.' Ben Short starts to curse, really blessed Parker out, and told him not him nor no one else was going to put him in jail."

"Then what?" queried an impatient listener.

"Well, I saw what would have to be done. Abe

Thomas was standing next to me, so I says let's help. Thomas went for the wagon, and Parker and I got hold to Short. He fought and kicked real hard, but we got him down and in the wagon and finally over to the jail. Parker told him plain he'd let him out in the morning when he was sober, and I know for a fact he went back several times that evening and during the night to check on him, make sure there was a fire in the stove and he was all right. You know Parker is the kind of man that'd do that."

Solemn nods of assent testified to Pa's character.

"I can't believe old Ben Short would shoot someone for locking him up. Still can't see how it came about," mused one of the men.

Now another took up the story. I was hearing about Pa the hero! "Well, Short got out of jail next morning, but his temper hadn't cooled off none. He was still mad and cursing, and he swore he'd get revenge for the disgrace on his family. Parker didn't take it serious, thought sure he'd cool off, but I told him I seen Short and heard him talking about how he was gonna get that blankety-blank James."

"Yeah, I did too," said another man. "Story was all over town by then. Heard Short say, 'I'll lay for him,' talk like that. 'Nough to scare a man, I'll tell you."

"A bunch of us went to Parker over to the store and warned him that Short was after him. I offered to tell Sheriff Green about it, but Parker wouldn't hear of it. I even suggested he go a different way home instead of right by Short's feed mill. But you know, he wouldn't let anybody bully him."

"Foolish pride, that's what it was," came another opinion. "Let stubborn pride walk him right into a trap."

I glared at the speaker who dared criticize Pa.

The other man continued his version of the story. "Well, he did take the precaution of walking down the middle of the street instead of right by the feed mill. Several of us kind of followed—at a safe distance, of course."

"And?"

"Well, he got right in front of the mill, and Short steps out and starts talking real ugly to him, telling him he brought disgrace on the family name and so on. Parker said *he* wasn't the one what disgraced the name. Short kept getting madder and madder, but Parker, he stayed calm. And all of a sudden, there was gunfire."

"Who fired first?"

"Can't say for sure. It went from words to bullets so fast, I never could tell. Sheriff says, though, Parker drew first. Sure beats me. Wouldn't have thought he would. Maybe he thought Short was going for a gun."

"Must be all them warnings made him a little

jumpy," suggested someone, but I didn't believe that my pa could be jumpy. Besides, if he shot first, how come Pa was the one wounded so bad?

"Parker's an awful quick draw when he wants to be. I seen him out practicing on tin cans. Can't believe he didn't get the best of it."

"His gun misfired on the first shot."

I nearly screamed aloud. Pa had been shot because of a fluke, an accident. I wanted to holler to God in Heaven that it wasn't fair. But I kept my peace to hear the rest of the story.

"Short, he stepped back inside and then commenced firing at Parker. There he was, caught in the middle of the street, with no shelter. He did fire back several times, and he hit Ben Short, you know."

Several murmurs of surprise hid my own gasp of delight. Pa had hit the man who shot him!

"It didn't last long. Parker was lying in the street, and we went to him as soon as we safely could. But it was rotten, the whole thing. And Sheriff says he's got to call it self-defense. Probably can't even arrest Short."

I wanted to scream aloud again.

"It weren't a fair fight," said Old Man Walsh, who had worked on a ranch in Arizona once, long ago, and still thought of the good old days of the cowboys and marshals. "Not like when a fellow faces his enemy right out in the open. Sign of what this world's coming to."

I felt proud of Pa but cheated. If the world were fair, my pa wouldn't have been lying inside dying. I kicked at a chicken that had wandered too close. It squawked and the whole group of men turned in one movement. They discovered me, of course, and one reached out and patted my head. "Poor child."

I turned and fled, not sure where I was going but just heading down the road toward town. After a bit, I stopped running and began to look around me. It was, I discovered, a wonderful day, with a warm breeze blowing and a clear blue sky that seemed to stretch past the far edge of town. Pa being shot and the men in our yard with their wild story seemed unreal and distant to me. Pretty soon, I found myself standing in front of the house of my one good friend, Florence.

Most of the girls in town were ladylike and proper, learning to sew and cook, and I didn't have much to do with them. But Florence was like me, a tomboy. We chunked rocks in the tank together and rode double on Buck and, to the despair of her proper banker father, walked barefoot in the rain down the middle of town one time. Florence got a hiding for it, but Pa told Ma never mind, I'd grow into a lady yet.

Florence had on a gingham dress with lace on it, and I knew right away her mother had stuffed her into it. Florence's way of getting back on such occasions was to sit in the yard and get it dirty, but there was a closet full of clean dresses inside and she usually just had to put another one on.

I pushed open the gate. Unlike ours, it didn't sag and offer to fall away from the fence. It swung smartly shut behind me, completing the neat white-picket barricade that set off the white two-story house and enclosed the grass and garden plots that, come spring, would boast bridal wreath, azaleas, and daffodils. Florence's father even had a gardener in to tend the yard. But right now Florence sat smack in the monkey grass.

"Hi," I ventured.

"Hi. Come sit down."

I sat next to her in the dirt. I didn't know what to say or why I was there, so I stayed silent. Finally Florence offered a comment.

"Must be pretty sad at your house."

"Yeah."

"Lots of people around?"

"My Aunt Nelda, and the Doc, and Brother Anderson. And then there's a bunch of men in the front yard."

"Aunt Nelda is probably more than you need."

"She is." I grinned just a bit. Florence understood, I thought, but her next comment cancelled out that idea.

"My ma says it's gonna be awful hard for your ma to support you kids. She says you don't have any money."

Anger swept through me, and I got up abruptly and left. We weren't the poorest folks in town, but we didn't have much either. Seemed like we always had to scratch. Florence lived in that big white house; ours was dirty gray and hadn't been white for years. Florence's family wouldn't have thought of keeping chickens in the yard, and they even had a lady come in to do the washing. But that's the difference, I thought, between bankers and dry-goods clerks. I didn't think it was fair of Florence to bring it up, though, and besides, she had spoken as though the dreaded possibility was a reality. Her words sounded as though Pa were already dead.

Aimlessly, I wandered back home, kicking pebbles and raising clouds of dry, red dust that settled over my shoes and stockings and even clung to the bottom of my dress that was supposed to stay clean another three days according to Ma's schedule. Twelve years old and skinny as a rail, with legs that grew too fast for even my seamstress-mother to keep my dresses long enough, I had only a few dresses, all made from hand-me-downs that had belonged to Ma or Aunt Nelda. I wore one dress for a week, then another; I was supposed to keep my everyday dresses very clean, but it went against my nature. Ma wrung her hands a lot. Today I kicked the dirt deliberately. I didn't want to go home to that house where every once in a while someone looked at me and said, "Poor, poor child," but there was nothing else to do.

3

Ben Short recovered from his wound, but Pa died two days after he was shot. I never did get to talk to him again. Oh, I snuck in a time or two when no one was looking, but Pa was never awake, and the last time he looked really bad. His skin was a funny color, and he was breathing loud—not snoring, exactly, but funny. It scared me, and I didn't go back again.

Aunt Nelda, of course, was the one who told us. She came into the room and matter-of-factly said,

"Well, he's gone," just as she might have said she thought it would rain. Doc Mason followed her, shaking his head either in grief over Pa or, more likely, disbelief at Aunt Nelda's attitude.

We all expected it, and yet none of us quite knew what to say now that the waiting was over. Ma sobbed quietly, and I did something I'd been wanting to do for two days. I ran over and put my head in her lap. She stroked my hair, all the time sobbing to herself, and I think she whispered once, "We'll be all right, Ellsbeth," but I never was sure because Aunt Nelda barged in.

"Bobby Joe's gone, Ellsbeth. You've got to go find him."

"Gone? Where'd he go?"

"I don't know," answered my determined aunt. "He just ran out the door like he'd taken leave of his senses." Then, with a touch of rare understanding, she added, "I suppose it's the news."

Ma reached out to me and said, "Ellsbeth, bring him home."

Suddenly I knew why B.J. had run off. The mere act of running would vent the grief that was welling up inside me. I burst through the door, took the steps in one bound, and rounded the corner of the house at a dead run, oblivious of the tears that ran down my cheeks and the wind that whipped at my legs, flinging my dress this way and that and exposing bare skin to its bite.

"B.J.! B.J.!" I called as loud as I could, and I could holler pretty good for a girl. The stock tank was my first thought. Where else would he have gone? But as I ran in that direction, I couldn't see him, and he didn't answer my shouts. I began to feel that cold wind on my legs and the blasts that blew my hair loose and tossed it in my face. A blue norther was rushing through, dropping the temperature so dramatically that the air itself was blue with cold. I stopped by the edge of the tank and looked around, hugging myself for warmth as well as consolation.

At the other side of the tank there was the beginning of a great thicket that surrounded a murky swamp. It was forbidden territory for us children because of snakes, the chance of getting lost, and just general dread on Ma's part. Standing there staring into that darkness I felt fear clutch at me. Would B.J. have gone in there? And would I have to venture into that haunted land to find him?

One last try. "B.J.? Please, B.J., answer me."

A slight movement off to one side of me was the clue I needed. There, crouched behind a bush, was my brother, tears streaming down his face.

"Go away, Ellsbeth."

"Oh, B.J., you had me scared. And Ma, too. What are you doing down here?"

"Can't you see?" he wailed. "I'm crying . . . and I . . . I can't do that anymore. I'm the m . . . m . . . man of the family now."

I stepped back a minute, then reached forward to touch him lightly. B.J. had to deal with something I couldn't solve, a wound I couldn't comfort, and I didn't think talking would help much. So we stayed there silent, him crouched down and me kneeling next to him.

But when the first needles of sleet hit me, I looked up and saw that the blue-gray sky was too dark for midafternoon. A whopper of a winter storm was coming, and we'd best run for home.

"Come on, I'll race you."

"No."

I turned my back on him deliberately and started for the house, every once in a while glancing over my shoulder to see if he was following. He was slowly putting one foot in front of the other, refusing to let the sleet and storm hurry him. I wanted to shout that I was freezing and for pity's sake to hurry up, but I somehow knew that I had to be careful and gentle with him, so I gritted my teeth and slowed my pace to his. But by now the sleet was steady and my dress was soaking wet. I was colder than I had ever been before.

The house looked warm and bright as we approached it, but I thought we would never get there. Uncle Charlie was on the porch, peering first in one direction and then another, looking for us. When he spotted our slow parade, he jumped off the porch and came to meet us, trying to scoop both of us up in his arms at once. We were too much of an armful, and he settled for hugging both of us, then picking B.J. up and telling me to run. B.J. resisted only slightly, then settled into those comforting arms, and I did as I was told. I ran for home.

"Where have you children been so long? Don't you know you had your poor ma half scared to death? And her grieving like she is!" Aunt Nelda held open the screen door, but she offered no comforting welcome.

"Nelda, these children are wet and cold. Get some blankets and dry them." Uncle Charlie sounded almost like a commander, and Aunt Nelda obeyed without saying another word. She came back in a minute with the blankets, handing one to Uncle Charlie and using the other to give me an awful rough rubbing down. When she got through, my skin sure did tingle with warmth.

Ma was holding Little Henry now, and she looked at us, asking repeatedly if we were all right. Doing much for us was beyond her right then, so Uncle Charlie was the one who took charge. I know he tucked B.J. and me into our beds, even though it was only midafternoon. We slept soundly.

It was dark when I woke up and I had no idea of what time it was, though I could hear lots of voices in the house. For a few minutes I snuggled down in the covers and listened to the wind whistle around the corners of the house. But curiosity was stronger than comfort, and I wanted to see what was going on. B.J. was still asleep, so I padded barefoot into the living room, careful not to wake him as I went.

They were all there—Uncle Charlie and Brother Anderson and Ma and Aunt Nelda and Uncle Fred. Ma's brother, our Uncle Jake Clemson, and his mousy wife, Aunt Thelma, had appeared while I was asleep. Aunt Thelma sat in a corner knitting and every once in a while glancing at Uncle Jake nervously. Just as before, no one saw me, and I stood quiet and took it all in.

Uncle Jake and Uncle Charlie were the center of attention, and they were having a whopper of an argument. Uncle Jake, as always, was trying to lord it over everybody, including Uncle Charlie.

"Charlie," he said in a carefully patient tone, "you can't possibly mean to transport this whole family clear up near Longview to bury Parker. We've got a family plot right here, plenty of room."

"Parker will be buried in our family plot." Uncle Charlie's voice had steel in it.

"Man, look at the weather. There's no way we can get up there."

"And," Aunt Nelda chimed in, "Lucille's not strong enough. Her condition, you know."

"You shush, Nelda. I'll take care of this." Uncle Jake frowned at Aunt Nelda, and she obeyed him for a minute. I guess he had that effect because he was her older brother. Anyway, she didn't give up easily. She went over and whispered something to Ma, but Ma didn't seem to be listening to Nelda or Jake or Charlie or anybody. She was still in her daze.

"I'll take care of Lucille," Uncle Charlie said quickly. He walked over to Ma and knelt down by her, speaking ever so much more gently. "Lucille, the funeral will be day after tomorrow, in Dalton Corners. I'll see that everyone gets there safe and sound."

Ma just nodded a little, and Uncle Charlie hugged her before he stood up. My mind drifted off for a moment to Dalton Corners. It was a little crossroad community near the farm where Pa had been raised. There wasn't much there except a store and a church, with the cemetery next to it. But Dalton Corners was home to the James family. It was where Grandpa and Grandma James lived and where Pa had a brother buried, one that died as an infant. Uncle Charlie was right, it was the place for Pa, but Uncle Jake didn't see it that way.

"Lucille"—his tone had more command than request in it—"you tell him. After all, you're the widow."

Just the sound of that word brought a fresh burst of sobbing from Ma, and she looked helplessly from one of them to the other, until Uncle Charlie took up the discussion again.

"Leave your sister be," he told Jake. "I've wired up to my folks to make the arrangements, and they're expecting us. The weather will clear by then, and that's the way it's going to be." And he deliberately turned his back, leaving Jake fuming.

Aunt Thelma had grown increasingly nervous during all this arguing, and she suddenly saw me as a way out. "Ellsbeth! Come, darling, you haven't had your supper. Let me take you to the kitchen."

I glanced at Ma to see if she was all right, but Aunt Nelda was fussing over her so much I couldn't get a good look, and I allowed myself to be led away. By the time Aunt Thelma settled me in the kitchen, B.J. was awake too, and we both had steaming bowls of vegetable soup. It tasted pretty good, and I ate more than I thought I would, but then I was tired again and kind of numb, and pretty soon

I found myself back in bed. I lay there and wondered at the way I felt. My pa had died, and I didn't know exactly how I was supposed to feel, but I wasn't sure I had it right. Sometimes I felt as if I ought to pinch myself to see if I was awake and everything was real.

There was no time for feeling much of anything the next two days. Everyone in Shelby County brought us food—turkeys and hens, potato salad and pots of beans and lots of cakes and some pies made from dried fruit. Aunt Nelda appointed me to kitchen duty, and I spent a lot of time serving food to all the people who came and went at the house. Luckily it was cold enough outside that I could put things on the porch and they'd keep. I really didn't mind working. It kept me busy, and I knew Ma couldn't do it. Seemed like every time I looked at her, she was sitting in that same rocking chair, with one or another of her family bending over her. Sometimes I would walk by and reach out and touch her, and she always squeezed my hand and tried to smile at me, but she was like somebody in a dream state. It was as if the feeling I'd had that first night Pa died, that numbness, had settled over Ma and never left.

I knew for myself that I couldn't be numb anymore. The longer I looked at Ma, the more I knew that B.J. had been right. He was the man of the house, and, for the time being, I was the head of the family. I sensed, I guess, that all of these people who filled our house now would be gone after the funeral, and then it would be just Ma, B.J., Little Henry and me—and someday the new baby. It didn't look to me as though anyone else could take charge, so I was it. I began by taking care of all that food.

The winter storm fooled Uncle Charlie. Contrary to his predictions, it raged for a day and a half, pouring freezing rain and occasional sleet down on us without stopping. I stayed in the house, hiding in the warmth of the kitchen, so that the weather didn't bother me. But Uncle Charlie spent lots of time staring out the window as though he were cursing the heavens for complicating his life at this bleak moment.

The day that Pa was to be buried dawned soggy and gray, but the rain had stopped. Uncle Jake wasn't the least bit gentle about it.

"There ain't no way a horse and buggy parade can get from here up to that country cemetery," he announced in a loud, I-told-you-so voice. "Roads are too muddy."

Uncle Charlie looked grim but said nothing and stared out the window. Then wordlessly he took his slicker and left. In about half an hour, he was back and had things all settled. I was awestruck by his efficiency.

"We'll take the noon train to Longview," he explained gently to Ma, deliberately ignoring Uncle Jake. "My father has made arrangements for buggies to meet us, and he says the roads are passable from Longview out to Dalton Corners. It will make the service a little late, but that's all right."

Ma nodded and seemed to be agreeing. I think Uncle Jake was tempted to announce he wasn't going, but he kept quiet. Aunt Nelda jumped into the fracas, though.

"Take these children and poor Lucille out in this dampness? Charles James, you can't be serious! They'll catch their death!"

Uncle Charlie wouldn't holler at her, because she was a lady supposedly, but he was pretty firm. "Bundle them up and they'll be all right."

That's what we did, bundled everybody up, even Little Henry. Nobody thought of separating children and adults or leaving children behind at a time like that, so Little Henry went along to the funeral. We took the noon train to Longview. I thought it was kind of exciting because we had only ridden the train once or twice before, but I knew it wasn't proper to enjoy it too much, so I had to poke B.J. every once in a while to keep him tamed down.

"Ellsbeth, look at these funny seats. What is this stuff? It prickles."

"Hush, B.J. I think it's called plush. Be real quiet, can't you, and just sit there?"

But he couldn't. "Look how fast we're going, Ellsbeth. Look at that barn fly by us."

And I would hush him again, but it did seem as though that barn and the whole countryside were flying by us.

The train was late getting to Center, and it was even later getting into Longview. The day being grim and stormy, it was pitch dark by the time we got to Dalton Corners. Lots of Pa's family from up around the area and people who'd known him when he was a boy and all kinds of others were gathered waiting at the cemetery for us, and they must have been there at least a couple of hours or more in that freezing cold.

As we approached the cemetery in the buggies Grandpa James had arranged for, the whole sky off to the east seemed to have an orange glow. B.J. and I were fascinated, but everyone was so quiet we were afraid to ask about it. Pretty soon, though, we rounded the corner of the church, and I drew in my breath sharp.

Grandma James was sitting next to me, a warm, big woman who was good at hugging, and I inched a little closer to her and hid my head on her comforting shoulder. It was a good long minute before I got the courage to look again, but I saw the same thing. There were ghosts or haints, like ones Ma said lived in the thicket behind the tank, and they were all standing and sitting around spooky, huge fires. The firelight danced on tombstones, and I could see the glow of lots of pairs of eyes in the light of the flames, but I couldn't make out any figures for real. All I could see were shapeless, formless figures with bright eyes. I clutched Grandma James.

I guess she knew what I was feeling, for she put out a big arm and circled me with it so that I felt safer. "Ellsbeth, look," she said softly, "the people have been waiting so long they've built fires and wrapped themselves in blankets to keep warm."

I screwed up my nerve to take a longer look, and, sure enough, I could make out people wrapped in blankets. They weren't haints at all! I felt better and followed Grandma James out of the buggy. When I looked at B.J. and saw he had a death grip on Uncle Charlie's hand and his eyes were as big as saucers, I felt even braver.

It took a few minutes to unload the coffin and get everything settled, and while we waited lots of people came over to us. They greeted each other as if they were on a picnic, with "How are you?" and "It's nice to see you again" and to B.J. or me, "My, how you've grown!" Oh, sure, some of them cried and lots of the ladies dabbed at their eyes with handkerchiefs, but many of them acted the way they would any other time. I wanted to shout, "It's my father's funeral! Don't you understand?"

The minister began the service with a long prayer, which left me lots of time to peer about at all the people. Most of them bowed their heads, and in the flickering firelight they looked like statues. That eerie feeling came over me again so hard I wasn't sure I was going to be able to sit quiet until the minister finished. I thought I might just burst with the funny feeling inside of me.

We all prayed together then and asked God to bless Pa for all his good and forgive him all his sins, which made me wonder, because I didn't think Pa had many sins. Then the minister told us what a good man Pa was and how sad it was that he had left all those little souls behind. I figured out that was B.J. and me and Little Henry, but it seemed a strange way to talk about us. Suddenly it struck me that this was the last time a lot of these people would know anything about Pa. I wanted the minister to stop talking about souls and honesty and devotion and all those big words and tell about the way Pa could make all of us, even Ma, laugh and how he took us swimming in the tank and how he wanted to be a rancher. But all the minister did was talk about his sins and his good deeds. Then we sang that hymn about Jesus walking and talking with us in the garden. The service was over before it seemed to me enough had been said.

The fires had begun to die down and it was awful cold, so people left as soon as the minister finished blessing us. They came up to Ma and hugged her or shook her hand and left. Ma sobbed and could barely look at any of them, but she managed to stand there as they filed by.

B.J. and I didn't know what we were supposed to do, so we stood and waited. There was a kind of family conference, with both sets of family getting together on it for once. Aunt Nelda seemed to be disagreeing, but Uncle Charlie and Uncle Jake actually shook hands on something, while Grandpa James nodded his head up and down in agreement. Then they all walked away as though a decision had been made.

Uncle Charlie went over and just picked Ma up and put her in a buggy, and Aunt Thelma followed carrying Little Henry. Before we could head that way, Grandma James came over to B.J. and me and said we were going home with her for a few days until Ma got settled down and then Uncle Charlie would come get us. That's what we did, and we never even said good-bye to Ma, but I guess she didn't miss us.

Our stay at Grandma's was like going from a world of darkness into one of light. She and Grandpa didn't talk about Pa at first, and they didn't pat us on the head and say, "Poor, poor children." But they fussed over us and gave us favorite things to eat—pancakes with warm syrup for breakfast and chicken-fried steak, the way only Grandma James could make it, for dinner.

The weather seemed to want to share in making B.J. and me happy. The first day we were at the farm dawned bright and clear, and by midday the temperature had warmed up so much we could be outside without being all bundled up.

Grandpa gave us a big bucket and said we could go down in the pasture to hunt for crawdads, and when Grandma warned me not to get my skirts muddy, he looked at her with a grin and asked, "Maude, don't we have an old pair of britches she could wear? Just this once, of course."

And Grandma found me a pair of britches, swearing me to secrecy because she said Ma wouldn't like it. I knew Ma would have raised holy Ned, but I also knew no one would tell her.

Feeling free as a bird, I raced B.J. to the pasture

and beat him by a good three lengths, even though I was carrying the pail.

"You wouldn't have beat me if you'd been wearing a skirt like you ought to," he complained, but I just laughed and threw a bunch of wet weeds at him.

We searched for crawdads, but of course we didn't find any, it being winter and all. I guess Grandpa knew we wouldn't when he sent us down there, but he also knew we'd have as much fun hunting whether we caught anything or not.

Another day Grandpa saddled his horse and a gentle mare he was specially fond of and took us riding all over the farm, showing us what he was planting and where Pa had shot his first squirrel and even the spot where the Klu Klux Klan had tried to hold a lynching on his property.

"Your pa was with me," he said. "He wasn't but sixteen, seventeen years old. Yet he helped run them hooligans off and save that poor black fellow they had. First time your pa ever pointed a gun at anything more than a squirrel, but he held it firm."

"Do you suppose he was scared?" B.J. was probably thinking how scared he'd have been, but I didn't want to hear about it if Pa was frightened. He was too much of a hero for me.

"Nope," Grandpa said to my relief. "He knew

anyone who hid behind a sheet had to be a coward. I was proud of him that day, and I'm still proud of him. He stood his ground when he had to."

We were silent for a minute, but then Grandpa asked me if I knew how to make my horse canter, and I told him, of course, Pa had taught me. So away we went, down the road that bordered one side of his farm, with B.J. behind Grandpa and me riding that mare all alone. The wind blew in my hair and the sun shone on my head and it was just grand!

We stopped to see a neighbor, about two miles down the road from Grandpa's house, because he wanted to ask about their little boy who'd been real sick. The farm lady tried to tell Grandpa how sorry she was about Pa and what a fine man she remembered he had been, but Grandpa just thanked her quietly and went back to asking what he could do for her or the little boy. She said he was getting better now, and then told us she'd put out some milk to clabber earlier and didn't we want bowls of clabber with sugar? We did and ate lots of it so we came back to Grandma's kitchen tired and full but awful happy.

I was sad when I saw Uncle Charlie coming down the road at the end of the week, even though I was glad to see him. He was back to his old humor and full of jokes, because he pulled up in front of where I was standing and stared at me.

"Pardon me, boy," he said, looking directly at my britches, "but I was looking for my niece, a nice girl who wears dresses. Have you seen her?"

I giggled in spite of myself and suggested he might find her about ten miles down the road.

"Why you little minx!" Uncle Charlie shouted as he jumped out of the buggy. "You're trying to send me on a wild-goose chase!"

I admitted my guilt, and he hugged me and asked more seriously how I was. I told him fine, and how was Ma?

"Oh," he said lightly, "she's gettin' on. She'll be all right. Come on, let's go see what Grandma has cooking." And he nearly dragged me into the house.

Uncle Charlie stayed a whole day at the farm, so we had an extra day of fun. The weather was still warm and balmy, and he took us fishing at a special place in the creek that he remembered from when he was little. Grandma promised to fry fish for dinner if we brought back some decent-sized catfish, but we caught only a couple of little ones, so small that Uncle Charlie threw them back saying they wouldn't be anything but bones. Still, it was glorious to sit on the bank and wait in breathless anticipation for a jerk on the line.

The next day Uncle Charlie put us in the buggy and took us home. I had to put on a skirt again, and Uncle Charlie smothered a grin when he saw me, then winked to tell me he'd keep my secret. B.J. and I kissed our grandparents and really meant it when we told them we'd had a wonderful week. They looked kind of sad, but Grandpa patted my head and said the mare would be waiting any time Ma would let us come back, and he told B.J. next time he'd have a pony for him. I think B.J. was kind of insulted that Grandpa thought he needed a pony, not a horse, but he thanked him.

And Uncle Charlie drove us away from that happy farm to a whole new kind of life.

4

Back in Center, I heard there had been an official investigation, leastways as far as such things went. Pa wasn't on duty, and he shot first or tried to, so the verdict was self-defense. Ben Short went free and back to his feed mill. Pretty soon folks forgot about the shooting, and his business never even suffered. Of course, there wasn't another feed mill in town for people to trade with. But that was how things were. Pa had been brave and right; Ben Short had been drunk and wrong, and he murdered my pa.

But he would go on with his life, and Pa was dead. There wasn't any justice. And in the backwoods of East Texas, there wasn't much law either. We had an opera house, but we didn't have a courtroom. All we had was a justice of the peace whom everybody called Judge.

After a spell, Ma went to work. It wasn't exactly a decision on which there was family agreement, but there wasn't much else she could do. We had to eat.

"I can get work as a seamstress. Mrs. Harper down the street has offered me a job before." She sighed and looked off in the distance. "I used to tell Parker I would take it, and he could give up being deputy sheriff. I wish now I had insisted."

"You can't go to work," Aunt Nelda announced. "You have children to care for. And, besides, the idea that my little sister should have to work for a living. . . ."

Uncle Jake, however, disagreed with Aunt Nelda and rode roughshod over her objections. I suspected that his motives had something to do with self-protection.

"Well, I sure to gosh can't support this family, too. Keeping up with my own is enough. You're right, Lucille, you're gonna have to work."

Aunt Nelda threw him a black look, and I didn't blame her. All the family he had to support was him and Aunt Thelma, and he had more money than the rest of us put together anyway. Uncle Jake could have fed us easily if he wanted to, but I'd have sooner lived on crow and squirrel.

Ma seemed resigned to working. "Ellsbeth is old enough to be a big help to me, and we'll get along. And, Nelda, you'll be able to help too, won't you?"

Shock flitted over Aunt Nelda's face. She was a lot better at ordering others to help than she was at doing it herself. And she sure wasn't much on such chores as dishes or diapering babies. She managed a fairly reassuring, "Oh, yes, of course."

Truth was, I was already doing all the housework, since the day Uncle Charlie brought us home from Grandma and Grandpa James's farm. Ma was waiting when we pulled up by the broken gate in the front yard, and she hugged us and tried to be brisk and cheerful. It didn't come off, though, because she kept dabbing her handkerchief at her eyes. Finally, as though to give herself something to do, she said she was sure we were hungry, and she'd just go out in the kitchen and fix a bite. I waited a minute before I followed her. She was standing in the middle of the floor, her face buried in her handkerchief, the most helpless figure I'd ever seen.

"Ma," I said, "you go talk to Uncle Charlie. I'll find something for all of us to eat."

And that's how I became a housekeeper at the

age of twelve, several years earlier than most girls. Ma had apparently stopped weeping while we were gone. It was just seeing us that sparked it again, and she soon got over it and started throwing us brave little smiles. But she didn't get over the helplessness that seemed to be part of her grief.

Ma worked from seven in the morning until seven at night, and she made seventy-five cents a day. It wasn't much, but it was enough for us to pay the rent and eat, though I had to learn to cook lots of beans and rice and to use leftovers every which way. It was easier without a man's hearty appetite to feed, but that was kind of a sad thought, and I used to push it from my mind.

We soon fell into a routine. Ma and I got up at six, and I fixed breakfast while she got ready for the walk to Mrs. Harper's house. Usually we had fried mush, though once in a while I would splurge and cook some of the eggs our chickens laid. Most usually, eggs had to be saved for the main course at supper. Anyway, while Ma ate her breakfast, I fixed her a lunch to take with her, and then she was off to work.

After she was gone, I had to get B.J. up and dress and feed Little Henry. B.J. was sort of a problem. I guess rebellion was his way of facing the change in our lives, but we never did get along too well in the mornings. I'd fuss at him to feed the chickens, and he'd dawdle and complain he couldn't find his other shoe and why did he have to do all the work? Sometimes I was tempted to remind him what he said that night at the stock tank, but I figured that wasn't fair, and I bit my tongue a lot.

One morning, however, I was out of sorts myself, and I lost patience with B.J. and forgot all about being fair. It was a dull, rainy winter morning, the kind that makes you feel too tired to do anything, and we were going to be late for school. I struggled with Little Henry and just about had him dressed when I saw B.J. was outside, climbing the Indian-sighting tree.

"B.J., you come in here right now." I stood at the door, holding Little Henry and fuming, while B.J. walked as slow as you please toward me.

"What now, Ellsbeth?"

"Did you finish your breakfast and bring in the wood?"

"Yep. I already done all my chores."

Well, of course, I went and checked on him, and he hadn't done anything. The chickens hadn't been fed, there was no wood in the stovebox, and B.J. had hidden his breakfast in the garbage instead of eating it. He hadn't done one thing right and what was worse, he'd lied to me. I saw red, and, without really thinking about what I was doing, I put Little Henry down and went and grabbed the switch that Pa used to keep on the back porch.

B.J. didn't see me coming, so I got in a couple

of good swats against his legs, good enough so I knew they hurt clean through his trousers. Of course, he yelped and cried and I felt bad, though I didn't let him know it. I'd threatened to take a switch to him a couple of times before but really doing it was something different, and I was kind of frightened by my own self. Yet I just acted stern the way Pa used to.

"There, B.J. James. Don't you ever lie to me again."

"I'm gonna tell Ma on you," he whimpered. "You ain't got no right to whip me. I'm gonna tell."

And he did tell Ma, first thing that night, as soon as she got in the door. Poor Ma was tired anyway, and here comes B.J. whining about me taking the switch to him. I stood silent, ashamed not that I'd switched him but that I'd done it in a burst of temper. Still, I kind of expected Ma to understand.

She let me down completely. In her prim and proper voice, she said, "Ellsbeth, I'm disappointed in you. You have no call to switch your brother. I'd hoped you could be more understanding of him."

Inside I was raging. Who, I wanted to ask, is understanding of *me*? "But, Ma, he lied to me."

"That's a very serious offense, and I'll take it up with B. J. later, but all you need to do after this is tell me. If there's any switching necessary"—she shuddered as she spoke—"I'll do it."

Ma herself used to switch at our legs, not as hard as Pa, but that was part of the change in her. She didn't have the force to discipline us. She never talked to B.J. about lying to me, and I knew that any other time I told her about something bad he'd done, she wouldn't do anything either.

Late that night, when Ma was in the parlor, I took the switch outside and hit it hard against the hackberry tree, over and over until it finally broke. It didn't make me feel any better, though, and I went in to bed and had a good cry.

Ma was always tired in the evenings when she came home, after sitting all days bent over a sewing machine and working the treadles with her foot. Sometimes she'd have a bad headache from straining her eyes to make the stitches fine, and I'd put her to bed with a cold rag on her head.

Other nights Ma seemed to realize she wasn't really taking her position as the head of our household, and she would try to play her role. "Ellsbeth, you wash Little Henry for me, please," she'd say, as though I weren't going to do it anyway. Ma would busy herself washing the dishes, but she was so tired that she often quit before she scrubbed the pots, and I would have to finish up.

Sometimes Ma would sit in a chair and sew tiny little garments for the baby that was coming. I'd be sitting next to B.J. at the dining table where we did our homework, and I'd stop studying to watch Ma. She was a fine seamstress, and Mrs. Harper used to give her leftover scraps. Ma used them to make baby clothes, and the only time she looked the least bit happy was when she was sewing these things. She knew the baby would be a problem, but I think she saw it as the last part of Pa that was left to her, and she really looked forward to its arrival.

"Ma, when will the baby come?"

"In the spring Ellsbeth, just about the time you and B.J. get out of school."

"What will we do when it starts to come? Will you tell me to boil pots of water?"

"Probably not." Ma smiled one of her brave little smiles. "I'll send you or B.J. for Doc and Aunt Nelda. They'll do what has to be done."

"Can we stay?"

"Hush, Ellsbeth. Of course not. You'll probably have to go to Aunt Thelma and Uncle Jake."

I gritted my teeth. I was grown up enough to take care of the house and children and Ma herself half the time, but I was to be hurried away when the new baby came.

"Ma?"

"Yes, Ellsbeth."

"What are you going to do about your job after the baby comes?"

She stopped sewing and stared off into space. "I don't know, Ellsbeth. I just don't know. I've been meaning to ask Nelda about that."

"Why do you always have to ask Aunt Nelda, Ma?" I couldn't keep the scorn out of my voice. And besides, Ma already knew how I felt about Aunt Nelda. "Why don't you just do what you have to without talking to her about every little thing? She's not always right."

"Shame, Ellsbeth! Nelda gives me good advice, and heaven knows I need help these days. And you shouldn't talk that way about your aunt." She bent her head to her sewing as if to punish me by her silence, but after a minute she went on. "Anyway, as I was saying, I could take a tiny baby to the shop with me and just stop working when I had to feed it. I don't think Mrs. Harper would mind. But the baby would soon get to be in the way. . . . I've been wondering about running a boardinghouse."

"A boardinghouse?" My voice squeaked with surprise. Boardinghouses were low class, run by tough old ladies, not someone frail and gentle like Ma. And I sure didn't want a bunch of strangers living with us.

"Yes, a boardinghouse. That would let me stay home with all of you and still bring us in some money. I'll talk to Nelda about it."

Nelda again! I gave up and went back to my studying.

Winter, such as it was, passed slowly with balmy spells interrupted once in a while by days of cold and rain, but we never had snow that year. I was too busy to chunk rocks, though B.J. went to the tank now and again, and I never even got to climb the live oak with B.J. to look for Indians.

"Please, Ellsbeth, let's play cowboys and Indians."

"B.J., what would I do with Little Henry? Besides, I've got to start supper. You go get me some more firewood."

"All the time I gotta do things like that," he grumbled, but he went and got the wood. I really ached to chunk rocks or play cowboys and Indians with him, which before I had always done just to please him, not really enjoying it much myself.

Florence had disappeared pretty quick after she found out how I was spending my days. Once she came by to see if she could ride Buck, and I explained Buck was gone. I didn't tell her we'd sold him for the money because her ma's comments about hard times at our house still rankled. Another time she asked if I wanted to walk to the railroad station and see if the next train wasn't the one that was carrying the circus up to Longview.

"Can't. I got to watch Little Henry, and I haven't done up the breakfast dishes yet."

"You have to do the breakfast dishes?" She was truly incredulous, and I hated her for it. Just because she had a maid and a ma who was at home, I bet she'd never washed a dish in her life.

"Sure," I said defiantly, determined she wouldn't guess how much I wanted to see the circus train.

I didn't miss Florence all that much, mostly because I didn't have time to do the kinds of things she wanted to do. Besides, I had a new friend who came closer to understanding me in those dark days. Her name was Lavine Abrams, and although she was a year younger than me, she was a whole lot older in lots of ways.

Lavine's brother, Isaac, had come to Center to take Pa's job in Wilkerson's Dry-Goods Store, and I heard rumors that he was real good at it, almost as good as Pa, but that some of the people in town weren't sure about doing business with a Jew and said so to Mr. Wilkerson. I was prepared not to like this Isaac just because he took Pa's place. It wouldn't have mattered to me if he'd been a Mormon, but it mattered to lots of folks in Center.

You see, there weren't many Jews in little towns in East Texas, and so Isaac was kind of a curiosity. No one would have been rude or mean to him or anything, but then again no one invited him to dinner or took him fishing or anything like that. They just kind of let him alone, and apparently it didn't bother Isaac too much.

But Isaac had this sister, Lavine, who came up from Galveston to live with him after he'd been in Center a short time. I knew about her and saw her at school, but I guess I was like everybody else in Center. It didn't occur to me to make friends with her.

Not till one day I overheard a whispered conversation that Florence was having with Alice Ruth Anderson, the preacher's daughter.

"My pa says they're tainted." She stage-whispered importantly, and Alice Ruth nodded her head in absolute agreement.

I came closer to listen. "Who's tainted?" I asked in a normal, everyday voice.

"Hush, Ellsbeth, she'll hear you!"

"Who?" I asked, having lowered my voice to the required whisper.

"That Abrams girl, that's who." Florence gave an obvious nod of her head in the direction of Lavine Abrams, who sat on a playground swing, all alone, looking kind of sad.

"Why're they tainted?"

"The Jews killed Christ, and they've been wanderers ever since." Florence spoke with a convincing air of authority, and Alice Ruth gasped with horror.

70

"Pa says," she went on smugly, "we best not have anything to do with them. Live and let live, he says."

I looked again at that lonely figure, just barely pumping as though she didn't even have heart enough to make the swing go. Suddenly I was angry at Florence and her pa and all the people in the world who were so uncaring. I knew what Pa would have said to Florence's father, and I said it to Florence.

"She's just like you and me, Florence Handley. Maybe a sight better." And I left those gossipy girls and walked over to plunk myself down in a swing next to Lavine.

"Hi."

She looked for a long minute, then soft as could be she said, "Hi."

"I'm Ellsbeth James."

"I know. I'm Lavine Abrams."

Well, it took some doing to get her to talk, but she finally did loosen up, and I asked her if she'd like to come home and have some cocoa when I fixed it for B.J. and Little Henry.

Afterward, Lavine came to the house most afternoons after school. It didn't surprise me too much that Ma was kind of like the rest of the people in Center. She thought it was good that I was nice to Lavine, but she wasn't sure I should bring her home with me. I just pointed out to Ma that Lavine was the only friend I had, the only girl who'd come keep me company while I did the afternoon chores.

Lavine kept house for Isaac, so she knew all about doing dishes and fixing supper and she understood when I had to do those things. The only difference was she didn't have other little kids like B.J. and Little Henry to take care of, so she had more time than I did, and she came to our house. She taught me how to cook some different things, beet soup and eggplant salad, and I tried to show her how to cook some of the things I fixed, like red beans, but she wouldn't eat them. She said the beans weren't kosher because they had pork in them. I did see, though, that she had her first taste of the watermelons that were Shelby County's pride.

We used to talk a lot those afternoons while I fixed dinner, and she told me all about coming from Russia on the boat and why they'd come and all.

"My mother said mobs used to come after us, so lots of the Jewish people tried to come to this country. Most of them went to New York, but somehow my family got on a boat that came to Galveston. It was all right, though, 'cause lots of people from our town in Russia were on the same boat. I just wish we had stayed in Galveston." Then she seemed afraid she had sounded rude. "Except, of course, that I never would have met you . . . but, anyway, Isaac couldn't find work there, so we had to leave our friends and come here." She stopped a minute, then went on, "And I'm glad I have you for a new friend."

I didn't ask Lavine why she lived with her brother and not her parents. I'd heard that story, and I figured she was worse off than I was. She'd lost both her parents and a little sister in the bad hurricane that hit Galveston in 1900. Only she and Isaac survived. At least, I had Ma and B.J. and Little Henry.

Ma got so she didn't feel real good all the time, and some afternoons she came home early from Mrs. Harper's. On one of those days, when she and Little Henry were both asleep and B.J. was off playing somewhere, Lavine and I sat on the front steps eating an early-spring watermelon and spitting the seeds.

"No, Lavine, you've got to spit them as far as you can. That's the whole point."

Lavine had never done anything so unladylike as spitting seeds, and she looked doubtful. But one thing I liked about her was she always would try something if I told her, and I was careful not to tell her anything real bad. This time she looked at me a long minute, watched me spit a seed as far as I could, then determinedly tried herself. And her seed went farther than mine! I laughed and laughed, and pretty soon I saw she had a grin, ever so little, but a grin.

"Try again," I urged.

She did, and the seed went sailing into the air, only to land right on top of Uncle Charlie's hat! We'd both been so busy spitting seeds—me laughing and Lavine grinning—that we'd never even seen him come down the road.

Uncle Charlie stopped dead still and very carefully reached up and got the seed and held it out in front of him, examining it wordlessly. He looked awful solemn, but I knew Uncle Charlie well enough to know he was going to burst out laughing any minute. If I hadn't happened to glance over at Lavine, it never would have occurred to me that she'd think otherwise. But the look on her face scared me. It was kind of like the expression of an animal that thinks it's going to be hit. She was cowering, trying to sink down into the steps, and she had her mouth open as though she was trying to say "I'm sorry" and couldn't get it out.

Uncle Charlie saw her about the same time as I did, and he immediately quit his act. "Lavine, it's all right. I'm not angry. I know you didn't mean it." Uncle Charlie was his most sincere, but even so Lavine stared suspiciously at the man kneeling in front of her. He had to talk some before she'd even sit up straight again, but trust Uncle Charlie! He had me laughing and her at least a little relaxed after a bit.

"There I was," he explained to the sky, "minding my own business and a watermelon seed hit me. Can you imagine?" He paused for his pretend listener to imagine, and then went on. "And the only people I saw were two lovely young ladies. Surely they wouldn't be spitting seeds. Never!" He shook his head as though the very idea horrified him, and I collapsed into giggles. Lavine looked uncertainly at me; then a funny little noise, like half a giggle, came out of her mouth.

Before long Uncle Charlie decided to show us just how spitting seeds really should be done, and there we sat, my big, grown-up uncle between us girls, all three spitting watermelon seeds.

And, of course, Ma caught us. A year earlier she'd have ranted, raved, and probably switched me, just before giving Uncle Charlie a piece of her mind. Now she simply said quietly, "Girls, I don't think you should do that." It was enough to make us stop right then.

"Charles, may I talk to you in the house?"

"Of course, Lucille." He gave us a secret wink. "Good-bye, ladies. We'll call the contest a draw."

After they left, Lavine turned to me with what for her was a big speech. "Ellsbeth, you don't know how lucky you are to be loved by so many people. Oh, I know you miss your pa . . . I really do know about the ache for people that have gone, but you have so much happiness, too. I like the way you laugh and do silly things like spitting watermelon seeds . . . and I . . . I envy you. I wish I could learn to be as happy as you are."

My first reaction was to be angry with her. Didn't she know I wasn't happy? But I knew that was wrong, and I sat there a minute thinking about what she said. I guessed that was something Lavine did for me. She showed me what was good about my life and made me thankful for what I did have, instead of spending all my time regretting Pa and all the work I had to do. But her saying so embarrassed me some.

"I gotta start supper," I said brusquely. "You want to come with me?"

5

Lavine and Uncle Charlie were all I had those days. That spring was a blur of housework and school to me. I seemed to go from breakfast and dishes to school to dinner and dishes, and then it was time to start another day and the whole round again. Nothing made one day stand out from another. Except the tornado. The day that storm came through Center stood out in vivid detail.

On that Saturday morning Ma was home, trying to help me with the housework and worrying me more than she was helping. B.J. came in with a load of firewood; he was always nicer about getting it for Ma than he was for me, and I didn't much blame him. He expected Ma to give him orders, but it was galling, I guess, to have to do whatever your sister told you. Anyway, he came in the door struggling under a huge load of wood.

"Boy, you should see the sky. It's green, like pea soup kind of."

Ma and I both went to the window and looked. Sure enough, the sky was greenish gray and the air was frighteningly still. Even the leaves on the trees seemed to hang in suspension, motionless. I walked out to the front porch to get a better look, and the air felt like a weight settling down on me. To the west, the clouds met the dark gray-green sky in a straight line, with little wispy tags hanging from it.

"Ellsbeth, you come in right now before you get exposed to that storm."

People believed just being exposed to some mysterious force in the storm would hurt you. I didn't believe it, but I didn't want to worry Ma, so I came in.

I no more than got back in the house when we began to hear this weird noise, like a train in the distance coming closer and closer. Then the hail hit hard. You hear stories about golf-ball-size hail, and I've heard some people swear they've seen hail as big as grapefruit. This seemed to me the size of one of those Shelby County melons I'd given Lavine to eat. It was huge and bounced off the roof and west windows of the house with such force that I was sure one of them would break. I made B.J. get under the crib, and not knowing what else to do with Little Henry, I put him in the crib and told B.J. to comfort him if he got scared.

Ma had gone out to the kitchen, and suddenly she screamed, "Ellsbeth! Help!"

My heart was in my throat as I shot across the hall from the bedroom to the kitchen. The door had blown open, and Ma, in her delicate condition, was trying to hold it shut. The force of the wind was too much for her, and the door kept flying open. She looked terribly frightened and exhausted.

"Ma, let me lean on it, and you go see if you can find the hammer and nails." I didn't lean, I pushed, but even so, I couldn't make the door stay shut, and I didn't see how Ma and I were going to nail it even if she did ever come back with the hammer and nails. It seemed as though she was gone forever, and all the time I stood there, counting to one hundred to keep my mind busy, I could hear this horrible roar outside.

Finally I heard Ma, near hysterical, saying, "Here's the hammer and nails."

And then the blessed sound of Uncle Charlie's

voice answered briskly, "Give them to me." I nearly cried with relief and terror mixing together when I saw him.

With Uncle Charlie's help, him doing most of the work and me helping push the door, we got it nailed shut. Then I remembered about exposure to the storm.

"Uncle Charlie, were you out in the storm? Did you get exposed?"

He put a protective arm around me. "No, Ellsbeth, I didn't get exposed. And I had to come and see if you all were safe."

As a matter of fact, he was more than exposed. He was out when the worst of the tornado passed by, and he was lucky to be alive, but I didn't realize that then.

Ma was just saying, "Oh, Charles, I don't know what we'd do without you," when Little Henry let out a horrible scream.

It was followed by B.J.'s frantic call, "Ellsbeth? Ellsbeth, come here, pl-e-a-se!" and I led the way as we all raced back into the bedroom.

I didn't know whether to laugh or cry when I saw Little Henry. He was standing in his crib screaming and pointing to the water that was pouring in on him. Directly above his crib there was a gaping hole where the roof had blown away. You could look up from his bed and see gray sky and rain.

That one hole wasn't the only damage. The whole roof suffered, and the chimney blew clean down. Yet even while we stood there looking the rain slacked off and the wind began to die.

Ma's reaction to the storm was mostly fright. After we had Little Henry settled down and Uncle Charlie had got the nails out of the door and left, she said to me, "Wasn't it a good thing Charles came to see after us? It just shows how much we need a man around the house, even if he is only a boarder."

I turned my face. I thought she'd forgotten all about that boardinghouse, but there it was again.

We were lucky, compared to others in Center. Mr. Wilkerson, who owned our house, had the roof and chimney repaired right away, and fortunately the weather stayed nice. Stories of the storm's damage filled the air for days, and you never knew how much to believe. There was a girl who died from exposure and there was a lady whose butter churn was carried by the wind for a block or two and then set down without a drop of milk spilling, and there was a baby found lying at the very edge of a stock tank, unharmed and holding its head out of the water.

We had proof that some of the stories were true. The back porch was torn off the house next door to where Isaac and Lavine lived, although not another thing was damaged. The lady who owned it lost all her preserves, which she'd had on the porch, and she carried on as though she'd lost a family member. Other damage was more serious. The twister ripped right through the school and demolished several rooms, my classroom among them. School was almost out for the year anyway, and the weather was nice enough so we generally met outside. When we couldn't, my class had to double up with B.J.'s class. I didn't like that at all.

And there were two children, younger than B.J. and me, killed when the storm passed through their farmhouse, some three miles from town. We all turned out for the funeral and grieved with the poor parents.

After the storm, the weather turned balmy and innocent, making the saying that East Texas is the land where the tall pines tickle the feet of the angels and the mockingbirds sing like nightingales seem true. Little Henry was toddling around by then, and I delighted in taking him outside to explore. I'd watch him with one eye and enjoy the heavenly day with the other. Lots of times, dinner was late because I spent so much time outside, but Ma didn't care and I ignored B.J. when he complained he was starving.

Most afternoons Lavine would come and sit with me, and we'd talk about the future and what we wanted from it. Lavine wanted to go back to Galveston, which didn't sound like much of a dream to me, but she insisted she wanted to marry "one of her own kind." She said she could work in some sort of a food store—delicatessen, I think—until the right boy came along. I had much grander ambitions, but they were a little vaguer. My fiercest wish was to get out of Center, and I was pretty sure after the last few months that I didn't want to get married and raise babies. But I wasn't sure what great thing I wanted to do. I didn't want to be a schoolmarm, and there wasn't much else. Sewing was out, and so was any kind of musical career. I plain lacked the talent.

"Maybe you could be a nurse," Lavine suggested one afternoon.

I remembered my last glimpse of Pa and discarded that idea quickly. "No, too much like keeping house. You end up taking care of people and doing the messy chores."

"You're running out of practical ideas, Ellsbeth." Lavine was always concerned with practical things, which was just what I wanted to escape.

"I know. But I'd really like to live way out West on a ranch."

"There aren't any cowgirls, Ellsbeth. You'd have to be a boy."

"There aren't hardly any real cowboys anymore, either," I added in dejection. My despair over my future was suddenly forgotten when I saw Ma coming down the road. She was walking real slow and looked kind of funny, so I handed Little Henry to Lavine and ran to meet Ma.

"Ellsbeth, you best call Doc Mason. I think my time has come."

"The baby?" Little shivers ran up my spine.

"Yes. Send Bobby Joe for Doc, and then tell him to get Aunt Nelda and to go on and stay at Aunt Thelma's."

"Do I have to go too?"

"Not yet, Ellsbeth. I may need you, at least until someone gets here."

Ma never noticed Lavine sitting in the corner of the yard, so I made a motion to her to keep Little Henry there. After I helped Ma into the house and sat her in the living room, I went off in search of B.J. He was down by the tank, and it was some time before I found him and sent him off. When I got back to Ma, she had put on a dressing gown and was lying on the bed. Every once in a while her face would twist up and she would kind of hold her breath, but other than that she didn't look any different from usual.

"They're coming, Ma. B.J.'s gone after them. Can I do something?"

"No, Ellsbeth, I'm all right. You go on and take care of Little Henry."

I didn't tell her Lavine had him, because I figured she wouldn't want an outsider around at a time like this, especially not Lavine. But I wanted her to stay.

I went out and whispered to Lavine, asking her to please stay because I needed company but to be quiet so's Ma wouldn't know. We brought Little Henry in the house and put him down for a nap. Then we both just sat in the parlor waiting for Doc Mason. Every once in a while we could hear Ma moan. She didn't cry out loud or anything, but she groaned and sometimes whimpered like a little puppy. I looked in on her once and she told me she was all right, but I thought she looked a little scared. I knew I was a lot scared.

It sure seemed to take Doc a long time to get there. I paced around the floor and kept peering out the window.

"What's taking so long?" I asked Lavine.

"Shh," she whispered. "He'll be here soon, and there's plenty of time. I remember when my little sister was born. It . . . it took a long time. . . ." Just remembering the mother and little sister she'd lost made Lavine sad, and she stopped talking a minute. Then she brightened. "And there's nothing to it, Ellsbeth. All you have to do is sit and wait."

I never was so glad to see anyone as Doc. He came in the door and stopped to talk to me before he went in to see Ma.

"Ellsbeth, you all right?"

"Yes, Doc. A . . . a little scared is all."

"Nothing to be scared of. Happens all the time. You want a boy or a girl?"

"Girl, I guess. We got two boys."

"Okay. Lavine, you keep her company," and he winked at Lavine and went in the bedroom to see Ma. He didn't stay too long, but Ma stopped whimpering while he was there, which I thought was a good sign. I considered leaning up close to the door to hear what was going on, but I was afraid Doc would come out fast and catch me or else Aunt Nelda would arrive.

She did arrive. First thing she said was, "Ellsbeth, you go on over to your Uncle Jake's. Thelma will watch after you. And take Little Henry with you. You'll just be in the way here."

Bless Doc Mason! He came out just in time to hear her and said in a booming voice, "Nonsense, Nelda. Ellsbeth's been taking care of this family, and she has every right to be here. She isn't a child these days, and you don't need to treat her like one. You'll take care of Little Henry, won't you, Ellsbeth?"

Just as I nodded, Aunt Nelda sighted Lavine,

who had kind of crept into a corner. She whirled around, still indignant that Doc had crossed her, and said to me, "Well, that girl can't stay here. The very idea!"

Doc interrupted again. "Lavine can stay because I gave her a special job to do." He winked at me this time, and I smiled ever so slightly.

Aunt Nelda stewed for a minute, then tried once more to take charge. "Ellsbeth, you go feed Little Henry."

"Yes, ma'am, but I usually wait until he wakes up to feed him." Lavine almost giggled, but Aunt Nelda didn't give up.

"Well, then, go boil some water."

"Yes," Doc said in a dry, funny tone of voice, "I'd love some coffee."

Aunt Nelda turned her nose up at all of us and strode indignantly into Ma's room where she spent the rest of the afternoon, occasionally sticking her head out to demand a cold rag.

The day seemed to drag on forever. Doc went in periodically to check on Ma, but he said there was no sense his sitting by her side every minute, and he even left for a while to see another patient. I was awful nervous when he was gone, and I was glad to have Lavine there to keep me from worrying. She ran home to tell Isaac where she was, but she promised to come back right soon. Lavine was good about letting Isaac know where she was every minute. Of course she was usually at our house, but she always told him. She said she didn't want him to worry, and I admired her for it.

The two of us fixed supper. Lavine made potato cakes, and I ground up some leftover meat for a loaf. Ma, of course, didn't want any, and Aunt Nelda declared herself too nervous to eat. but Doc and Little Henry and Lavine and I had a good supper, except Lavine wouldn't eat the meat loaf.

After the dishes were done, we settled down in the living room to wait. Ma's cries seemed to be getting louder and closer together, and even though Lavine and I tried to think of a way to get me to a ranch, it was hard to concentrate on the future with Ma having a baby in the next room. Besides, I didn't like Lavine's opinion that probably the only way I was going to get to live on a ranch was to marry someone who owned one.

Suddenly a loud, wailing cry cut through the night.

"That's the baby," Lavine whispered, wearing a big smile.

I rushed to the bedroom door, then stopped, afraid to knock or anything. I guess Doc knew, because he called out to me.

"Ellsbeth? It's a girl. You wait just a minute, and then you can come in and see both of them."

Lavine came up to me and took my hand. "I'm awful happy for you, Ellsbeth. Baby girls are"—she kind of choked and went on—"baby girls are fun. I've got to go now." And she ran out the door before I could even thank her for staying with me.

Doc finally opened the door and said, "Ellsbeth, you can come in and see these girls for a minute. Then would you get me some more coffee? It's late, and I've got a call to make yet."

"Sure, Doc," and I tiptoed into the room.

"Ellsbeth, now don't you tire them out. You can't stay but a minute." Aunt Nelda was standing guard like a watchdog.

"Nelda," Doc said, just barely holding on to his patience, "you get out of here and get the coffee for me. And leave Ellsbeth alone with her ma."

I stared down at Ma. She was holding this red, funny-looking baby in her arms, and I tried desperately to think of something nice to say. I just couldn't come out with "She's pretty" or any of the things I thought I ought to, so I said, "You all right, Ma?"

"Yes, Ellsbeth. Just very tired. Isn't she pretty?"

"Yeah," I gulped. "What's her name?"

"Margaret Ann. Your pa picked that name." Ma closed her eyes, just as if I wasn't there, and after a minute I tiptoed away.

And that's how Maggie came to join our family.

It was sort of like taking another passenger into a leaking boat, and I worried about that baby. If I'd had any sense, I guess I'd have worried about myself, too.

6

Ma did go back to Mrs. Harper's a couple of weeks after Maggie was born, but the hours were hard on her and she worried about taking too much time with the baby, though far as I know Mrs. Harper never said anything. No matter, Ma was set on having that boardinghouse. They say sometimes when people are grieving they make a lot of bad judgments. This was sure one of Ma's.

"Your Uncle Charlie came by Mrs. Harper's today to see me," she said one evening.

"He did? Where's he been? Why hasn't he come to see us?"

"Says he's been in Dallas. I think maybe Charles is planning to go into business or something. Now that he's the only James son, he's turning more responsible." She paused just a minute, then went on. "I talked to him about our boardinghouse."

Uncle Charlie had indeed turned responsible since Pa died, so responsible that I was sure I could count on him to squash the idea of the boardinghouse.

"Didn't like it, did he?"

"No, Ellsbeth, he didn't."

My sigh of relief came too soon, though, for she went on. "But he said if I was bound and determined, he'd help me."

"Ma, *are* you bound and determined?"

"Yes, Ellsbeth, I am. The hours at Mrs. Harper's are too long, and you children aren't getting the attention you need."

"We're getting along, Ma."

"Not like you should."

There was no use talking to Ma. I could tell from her tone of voice she had her mind set on that boardinghouse.

I wanted to kick Uncle Charlie in the shins when he appeared after supper two or three days later to announce that he'd found a house that would be suitable for a boardinghouse.

"You mean we'd have to move from here?" I couldn't believe what I was hearing. Give up the stock tank and the chickens and the nearby stands of pine?

"Ellsbeth, my love, you are a dunce." Uncle Charlie ruffled my hair affectionately, but I was in no mood to be petted and I drew away. "This little house isn't big enough to take in boarders. And it would need too much repair before anyone but you would want to live here."

"Hush, Ellsbeth, and let me hear about the house."

"It's the Banks house across town. You know, that old lady died some time ago and the house is vacant. Well, I talked to the lawyer, and he said he thinks the heirs will lease it. They live in Dallas, so I called on them while I was there, and they might consider leasing it to the right party."

The other side of town! By my way of figuring that was the wrong side of the tracks, closer to Florence and farther from the stock tank. The fact that the Banks house backed up to a thick stand of pines did little to comfort me. I listened with a black scowl on my face.

"Is it close enough to town, Charles?"

"I think so. Your boarders might have to walk some, but it's an easy walk."

"How big is the house?"

"Big enough. There's four bedrooms upstairs and, what with the parlor and sitting room and all, enough room for you and the children to live downstairs. You can rent out the whole upstairs."

"Would I make enough money? How much should I charge a boarder?" Ma looked puzzled. She never had been much good with money, and Pa had always taken care of things like that.

"I calculated on that, Lucille, and I figure you can ask seven and a half a month, if you give them breakfast and supper. That's thirty dollars a month all told."

Thirty dollars a month sounded pretty good to Ma, I guess. "Charles, would it work? We could begin with the new schoolteacher that's coming to town, I suppose."

"Okay, Lucille, but the new teacher's a man, and I think you'll either have to have ladies or men but not both, what with the arrangement of the house. So you'll have to take men boarders."

"I guess I would want to, Charles. We need a man around the house just to make us feel safe."

Uncle Charlie went back to Dallas and made a commitment for Ma to rent the house for one year, beginning in July. The people were real nice and said she could pay the first month's rent after we got settled with the boarders, so it would be almost like free. Ma was pleased, happier than she'd been since Pa died except for when Maggie was born, but I had a sinking feeling she didn't know what she was getting all of us into. I particularly saw myself cooking huge pots of beans and rice.

Uncle Charlie took us to inspect the house, and I had to admit it was prettier and brighter than home. And it was lots bigger. The Banks house was furnished, and we were going to get rid of all but the best of our stuff, most of which wasn't near as nice. I began to take heart.

B.J. was delighted. He seemed oblivious to the loss of his Indian-sighting tree and the stock tank and saw only that the new house was closer to the school, so he could play ball in the school yard with his friends. And it was closer to town, so he wouldn't have to go so far when he got sent on errands. I thought he was shortsighted, trading unimportant things for the real special good of our old house.

Ma said we had to be moved in and settled before we could advertise for boarders, so our first job was to pack up the house. As usual, Ma got tired pretty quick.

"Ellsbeth, you just pack up the rest of these dishes. I'll check on Maggie and lie down for a minute. Where's Little Henry?"

"Outside, Ma. I told B.J. to watch him."

"Oh, I don't know if that's good. B.J. might let him wander down to the tank. I'll be so thankful when we're away from that tank. You better bring Little Henry in here with you."

How was I supposed to pack dishes and watch a walking curiosity stick at the same time? I did, and I blessed myself out for being angry about it. It wasn't that Ma was lazy. She just seemed to have lost the spark of life, and my part was to help her.

One thing Ma didn't ask me to do was sew. She knew my clumsy fingers, and she let me pack while she worked on linens for our boarders. It would have been lots easier if Ma had a sewing machine, but we never had been able to afford one and she had to do it all by hand. Her needle fashioned sheets and pillowcases of the muslin Mr. Wilkerson had given her at discount, and she and Aunt Thelma made two more comforters to supplement the supply we had.

"You know, Lucille," Aunt Thelma spoke tentatively, "you will have to wash clothes frequently. All this linen!"

"That's right, Lucille. It's going to be too much work. Even with Ellsbeth to help you!" Honest to gosh, Aunt Nelda was just sitting there watching Aunt Thelma and Ma sew and me pack, but she felt privileged to criticize even if she didn't help.

"It will work out, Nelda. Ellsbeth and I realize it's going to be hard."

Did I realize! I listened to Ma's calm conviction that it would work out, and I suddenly understood something about her. Ma was so wrapped up in her own world, with the new baby and still missing Pa, that she didn't know all the problems we faced. She assumed the boardinghouse would work, even though she hadn't given one practical thought to the cooking and washing and cleaning it would take. Pa used to tease her about being so practical. He'd have fainted if he saw her now! The boardinghouse would work only if someone would come along to help her. That was how Ma was these days, so helpless that she needed a guardian angel.

For a while, as we got ready to move, I thought Uncle Charlie was that guardian angel. In fact, I even hoped that he would become one of our boarders. But he surprised us all one day when he came back from one of his trips to Dallas.

"I'm going to be leaving Center, Lucille," he told Ma, not us children, "and I'm a little concerned about leaving you and the children. Of course, there's Jake and Nelda. . . ."

"Oh, Charles!" There was real dismay in Ma's voice. "Why are you going? And where?"

"I've taken a position with the railroad in Dallas, but . . . ah . . . there's a special reason."

This was an adult conversation, but nobody had told me to leave the room, so I felt it would be permissible to ask, "What special reason, Uncle Charlie?" I was already devastated that he was leaving, abandoning us to the mercy of the Clemson side of the family.

"I'm going to be married. That's . . . it's the real, I mean, she's the real reason I've been going to Dallas on the train all those times."

"She?" I was downright disgusted. Some unknown lady was going to take Uncle Charlie away from us.

"Her name's Annabelle Matthews, Ellsbeth, and you'll like her. She's kind of like you, as a matter of fact."

"Who's like Ellsbeth?" B.J. came running into the room. "Does she chunk rocks and cook supper and boss boys around, whoever she is?" He ducked as I reached out to swipe at him.

"No, but she's spirited like Ellsbeth. You'll see. I'll bring her to Center."

I wondered how you could like anybody named Annabelle.

Ma kept asking Uncle Charlie all these questions about how they'd met and when the wedding was and so on, but I left the room, too downcast about losing Uncle Charlie to care how he'd met this Annabelle.

Uncle Charlie stayed in Center long enough to

see us settled in the new house, because I guess he knew Uncle Jake and Aunt Nelda were better on offering opinions than doing anything. Uncle Jake came to supervise, and he even had the nerve to tell Uncle Charlie where to put the few pieces of furniture we brought with us. But Uncle Charlie was the one who hired the dray and moved most of the stuff.

"Ellsbeth, how do you like your house?"

"It's better than I thought," I admitted reluctantly, looking at the bright sunny kitchen that would be my world. Sunlight filtered through organdy curtains and landed on the floor in great squares. There was a round oak table in the middle of the floor and an old rocker in the corner that would be perfect for soothing Maggie. And there were lots of cupboards low enough for me to reach. In the other house, I'd always been having to drag a chair over to get to something high up.

"Come on, let's take a tour through," Uncle Charlie suggested, and we wandered from room to room. The shelves had been taken out of the pantry off the kitchen, and it had been made into a bedroom for B.J. and Little Henry. It barely held a bed and crib, but Ma said they wouldn't do more than sleep there and it would be all right. The parlor had become a huge bedroom that Ma, Maggie, and I were to share, and the sitting room would be for all our family. It looked warm and inviting with mahogany chairs and velvet drapes and a velvet rug on the floor. The last room Uncle Charlie and I looked at was the dining room, which was almost filled with a huge, long dining table, big enough to feed the boarders. There was only room for one sideboard with the table, but Ma had hung some prints on the wall and put Japanese matting on the floor, and it looked real nice. We were in the boardinghouse business for real!

But we lost Uncle Charlie. He left for Dallas two days after we moved into the new house and was to be married the next week. Ma would really have liked to go, and I would have too, mostly so I could see Dallas. But of couse we couldn't, and Uncle Charlie knew it even when he invited us. Later he sent a long description of the wedding, telling us that it was a simple ceremony with just a few of Annabelle's family. Her sister sang, "Oh, Promise Me," and her brother broke down and cried, which was a pretty dumb thing for a boy to do, I thought. There was a wedding breakfast at some big hotel afterwards, and they ate quail of all things! Quail was pretty ordinary to me. It was what you had to pick shot out of and eat after your pa or one of your uncles went hunting, and I'd have thought they'd have chosen something fancier for a wedding breakfast. My doubts about Annabelle grew.

Ma got sort of teary-eyed when she read Uncle Charlie's letter. "It sounds lovely, doesn't it, Ellsbeth? When your pa and I were married, we had a beautiful wedding. Miss Richardson from the church sang "Oh, Promise Me," just like at Uncle Charlie's wedding, and the cape jasmines were in bloom and the church was filled with them. . . ." Her voice drifted off and she sat for a long while, obviously reliving a happier time in her life.

"Ma, there's a gentleman at the front door. I think . . . I guess he wants to inquire about rooms."

That was one way to bring Ma back to the present in a hurry. She had put an ad, very small and proper, in the newspaper recommending our clean rooms and excellent food. Now the first possible boarder was at our door. I viewed him as an enemy to be conquered and turned away.

To my dismay, Ma said, "Ellsbeth, you show him the rooms." She hesitated a minute. "But . . . I guess after you show him, I'd better talk to him."

So I went back to the door where the man stood waiting. He seemed old to me, probably at least thirty, and he was in work clothes. His face was tanned, as if he worked outdoors, and his hands rough. He'd told me his name was Beaver.

"Thanks, little miss." He was kind of hearty and smiled a lot, and I almost liked him.

I showed Mr. Beaver the four rooms upstairs. They were all corner rooms, pretty much alike with windows on two sides, one giant closet and plain furnishings—an iron bedstead, a chest of drawers, one comfortable chair, and a table and chair to serve as a desk.

"These all look mighty fine to me, little miss, after the tents I've been living in."

"Tents?"

"Yes, ma'am. When you work in the oil fields, that's what you live in. Tents."

Oil fields! Good gravy, I thought, I hope Uncle Fred doesn't ever find out. He'd pester Mr. Beaver to death.

"I believe I'd like that room on the east. I like to see the sun comin' up of a morning."

So I took Mr. Beaver down and introduced him to Ma. She didn't seem to know much about interviewing boarders, and I wasn't sure what she expected to find out. Mr. Beaver told her, as he'd told me, that he was from the oil fields, and Ma recoiled a little.

"The oil fields?" she echoed faintly.

"Yes, ma'am, but that's too rough a life and not much money for the likes of me. I've taken a job here in Center."

"Oh. You do have employment then?"

"Yes, ma'am. A good job. And I'll make you a

good boarder. Won't cause no trouble or make no noise. I just want a clean place to hang my hat."

And that was how Will Beaver came to be our first boarder. B.J. took an instant shine to him, for he was a happy and patient man. He even had time to pitch washers with B.J. in the evenings after supper, and once or twice he took him fishing. I was tempted to like Mr. Beaver, who continued to call me "little miss," but I was too busy for the fishing expeditions.

Uncle Jake didn't like Mr. Beaver at all. "Riffraff from the oil fields! That's what you've let in the same house with your children, Lucille."

Ma didn't stand up to Uncle Jake the way Pa used to. "The children like him fine. He seems very nice, Jake."

"The children like him fine," Uncle Jake mimicked. "What do they know about people? I tell you I know people when I meet them, and that one's no good."

As Uncle Jake left, he met Mr. Beaver in the hall and issued a threatening warning, "You leave this family alone, you hear? They're under my protection, and I'm not far away!"

With that, he stomped out of the house, leaving Mr. Beaver staring after him with a puzzled look on his face. After a minute, he knocked on the sitting-room door.

"Mrs. James? Could I see you a minute?"

"Yes, Mr. Beaver. What is it?"

"Ah, ma'am . . . ah, your brother . . . is something troubling him?"

"He thinks you're out to rob and murder us," I blurted out, much to Ma's horror.

"Ellsbeth! No, Mr. Beaver, nothing serious is troubling my brother."

But Mr. Beaver took my word over Ma's. "If there's going to be any trouble. I'll just move out. I wouldn't want to worry you none . . . and, to tell the truth, I don't want to mess with people like that."

"There'll be no trouble, Mr. Beaver," Ma told him, but I knew she wasn't sure. There was no telling what Uncle Jake would do.

Ma looked to Aunt Nelda for support as usual, but once Aunt Nelda heard Mr. Beaver was from the oil fields, she too was horrified, mostly I suppose because of Uncle Fred. They both happened to be in our sitting room when Ma brought the subject up, so Uncle Fred heard the news and immediately went off in search of Mr. Beaver, leaving Aunt Nelda behind to rant and rave.

"A roustabout or roughneck or whatever they call them! Lucille, how could you?"

"He's not a roughneck," I chimed in. "He's a very nice man, just as respectable as the rest of us."

104

"Children should speak only when spoken to," intoned Aunt Nelda.

Ma stood her ground this time. She had to. Mr. Beaver was the only boarder we had, and she didn't want to lose him. We'd already spent the seven and a half he had paid in advance, and if we asked him to move, we'd have to return it.

"Nelda," Uncle Fred interrupted, as he came back from talking to Mr. Beaver, "you know, I might just go down around Beaumont and have myself a look-see at what's going on."

"Fred Dawson, I will not go to Beaumont."

"I didn't expect you to," he said mildly, and I cheered silently, turning my face so Aunt Nelda wouldn't see my grin. I hoped Uncle Fred would really carry through and go to Beaumont. Just to see the oil fields would make him happy, and heaven knew he deserved some happiness.

"Now see what you've done," Aunt Nelda accused Ma.

In the end, Mr. Beaver stayed and was joined by two more boarders, both of whom gained the approval of Uncle Jake and Aunt Nelda more easily. B.J. and I didn't like either one half as well.

One of our new boarders was a man from Longview who'd been hired to keep the books at Ben Short's feed mill. His job was difficult for Ma to accept, because anything connected with Ben Short was painful to her. She still referred to him as the man who murdered Pa, and she wouldn't even speak to his wife on the street. But Mr. Andrews was an inconspicuous, quiet old man, and Uncle Jake insisted Ma was being silly, that Mr. Andrews had been safely up in Longview when Pa was shot and was simply at the feed mill to do a job. As usual, Ma gave in to Uncle Jake and accepted Mr. Andrews as a boarder. After all, we needed his seven and a half. Ma never did like him, though, and was always coldly polite to him at the dinner table. I didn't like him because his false teeth clacked and he kept patting me on the head.

The third boarder really irked B.J. He taught B.J.'s class at school, or anyway he would when school started again in the fall. Mr. Eastman was a tall, skinny man with a bald head. He spent a lot of time in his room, preparing lessons he said, and he went for occasional walks around town to acquaint himself with it, he explained. At the dinner table, he sometimes quoted poetry, and then he'd smile at B.J. and assure him he'd enjoy reading Longfellow in school.

"Who is Longfellow?" B.J. whined to Ma one night, after the boarders had left the dinner table and we were clearing up.

"He's a famous American poet. I'm sure Mr. Eastman is right, B.J. You'll enjoy reading his poetry."

"Fat chance," B.J. muttered.

I chimed in too. "Ha! I had to read it last year and it's silly. You'll love the pitter patter of little feet and all that, B.J." I picked up a tray full of dirty dishes and headed for the kitchen. "It's between dusk and dark now. Is this the pause in the day's occupations known as the children's hour?"

It was a mean thing to say, and I'd said it deliberately, but Ma looked so stricken I could have bitten my tongue off.

"Ellsbeth, you go out and play. I'll do the dishes."

"Oh, Ma, I didn't mean that. I was just teasing B.J." A little white lie wouldn't hurt, I reasoned, as I hurried into the kitchen before Ma could see the tear rolling down my cheek.

B.J. followed me. "Ellsbeth, why don't you come out for a little while? Mr. Beaver might play ball with us. He's been teaching me how to throw the right way, and I bet he'd show you."

"Can't, B.J. I really better help Ma with the dishes." I turned away quickly so B.J. wouldn't read on my face how mad it made me to have to stay inside. But I couldn't rid myself of that bottled-up feeling, and when Ma's good ironstone platter jumped from my hands and shattered on the floor, I honestly didn't know if it was an accident or not.

That was kind of how running a boardinghouse

was—lots of work. I washed so many dishes and clothes and cooked so many dinners that most times I was too tired to play even if I had the time. And Ma wasn't a whole lot of help. She didn't have any stamina. Some days she'd work real hard for a while and I'd think she was beginning to get over her grief, but then she'd have spells of bad days when she just couldn't seem to do anything, not even decide what to fix for dinner. Maggie took a lot of time, and Little Henry was at the age where he was a real terror to look after. What it amounted to was that if I was doing housework, Ma had to look after the babies, and if she did the housework, I watched them. There was a blessed period just after noon dinner when they were both asleep and we didn't have to worry about them, but it always seemed too short.

B.J. had chores, too, of course, like bringing in the wood and putting fresh water in the wash pitcher in each room and doing the yard work, but he wasn't much good with Little Henry. One time he let him wander off about two blocks and Ma nearly had hysterical fits till we found him. Afterward, she never let B.J. take care of Little Henry again.

Lavine was about the only company I had. She'd walk over to our house in the afternoon and sit and hull peas with me or peel potatoes or help with whatever I was doing. Sometimes, if Isaac was going to work late, she'd stay to supper—though she was real careful about what she ate—and once Isaac let her spend the night. Ma didn't like it much, but she helped us make mattresses out of blankets and we put them on the sitting-room floor. We lay on them there and talked far into the night.

Ma came to the door once. "Hush, girls, you'll be tired in the morning."

"Yes, Ma." We waited until we could hear she'd gone back to bed, and we began to whisper again.

Ma was right. Morning came too quick and early, and we were awful tired as we went about the breakfast chores. But I was glad I had Lavine for a friend.

Florence came around once, saying she was glad I lived so close and did I still have to wash dishes? I told her yes, but she could come talk to me while I worked. She tried that, but it didn't work very well. I didn't like what she said and told her so.

"How come that Abrams girl is here all the time?"

"She's my friend."

"How can you have one of them for a friend? My pa says they're all alike . . . and Ma says next you'll be taking up with a nigger girl."

"Florence Handley, that's a mean thing for your ma to say, and for you to repeat." I was really angry. "Lavine is a better friend to me than you ever were, and you can tell your ma I said so. You're the one that's tainted . . . with ugly ideas about people."

She never said a word, just kind of stuck her head up a little and headed out the door. Just before she left, though, she turned and issued what she thought was a terrible threat, "Ellsbeth, I won't ever come back here again."

"Good," I screamed after her. "Go away and stay away."

I never saw her after that. We didn't even speak at school. Lavine asked about it once, but I brushed her question aside and never did tell her. I figured she guessed anyway.

I've read sometimes about a summer that flew by on golden wings of something, maybe fun or play or swimming. Time flew by for me, too, but its wings weren't golden. They were more dishwater gray. For me, that year was like a year with no summer. I worked from morning to night. I couldn't believe three additional people could make that big a difference in the work, but they did. And I worried about how Ma would manage when fall came and I had to go back to school.

"Ma, I think I better not go to school this year. You can't manage by yourself." I had to force myself to make the suggestion, because I loved school and I hated the thought of not going back.

"No, Ellsbeth, your pa believed in girls getting a good education, and you're going to school."

"You're sure?"

"I'm sure."

"Yes, ma'am." I obeyed with relief.

We never did get a fourth boarder by the time school started, though Ma occasionally ran that tiny ad about our clean rooms and good food.

Then one day I came in through the kitchen from school and Ma, her face kind of aglow, was making chicken-fried steak for supper. Now chicken-fried steak is a lot of work, and we rarely fixed it. Certainly Ma never fixed it herself. But here she was with pans full of hot grease ready to fry the steak she had floured.

"Ellsbeth, we have a new boarder."

I wasn't too interested, but I pretended. "Really? Who?"

"His name is Millard, Joseph Millard, and he's a fine gentleman. He's come from Colorado City to Center to work in the bank."

There's something about banks that automatically confers respectability on those who work in them. I could see that Ma was impressed, and I knew the new boarder was the reason we were getting chicken-fried steak. If Ma was that enthusiastic, I'd try to be too.

I met Mr. Millard at dinner that night, and I instinctively disliked and distrusted him. It was one of those feelings I can't explain, just something I knew.

While Ma introduced him to the other boarders

and went on about how pleased we were to have him with us, Mr. Millard smiled, but he smiled mostly at Ma. Then he shook hands with the other boarders, but he still kept looking at Ma a lot of the time. I studied Joseph Millard from his head full of dark hair to the tips of his perfectly polished shoes. He did have a whole lot of hair, but he combed it in neat waves, the kind that were fashionable back East, so we heard. And he had heavy, dark eyebrows that seemed to accentuate his eyes. He was very respectable looking, dressed in a clean white shirt with a celluloid collar and a neat suit without a wrinkle in it. Next to him, Mr. Beaver, in his work clothes, looked like the roughneck Aunt Nelda thought he was. Mr. Millard was the kind of man you hear ladies giggle about, saying he makes their hearts flutter. Not mine. I didn't like him.

Ma saw me staring at him, and when she introduced me, she eyed me sharply to see that I was polite. I was, of course, and Mr. Millard smiled real hard and said something nice about how lucky I was to look like Ma, and then he smiled at Ma again and she kind of blushed. I knew he was just trying to say the right thing because Lord knows I didn't look pretty like Ma, but I wouldn't have resented his white lie from someone else. I disliked *him*, not what he said.

7

A day or so later, we got a letter from Uncle Charlie saying he and Annabelle would be in Center in two weeks. At first, I thought that wasn't long at all, but it turned out to be a never-ending two weeks during which my dislike for our newest boarder was equalled only by my amazement at everyone around me. I couldn't wait for Uncle Charlie to arrive, because I knew he'd agree completely with me about Mr. Millard.

That man was absolutely charming, and I despised

him. He always smiled, and he always had some polite, nice thing to say to you. "Ellsbeth, how was school today?" Those black eyes would look right at me, and he'd smile so hard the corners of his mouth nearly reached to his ears or at least it seemed so to me.

"Fine," I'd mutter and turn away, but he acted as if he never noticed my attitude. He'd just try again another day.

One evening he came in and sat at the dining table where I was doing my studies. He didn't say "May I interrupt you?" or anything; he just started talking or, really, asking.

"Ellsbeth, someone at the bank today told me you used to live across town, out in the country."

I nodded, scribbling madly so he'd get the idea I was busy and go away. But he kept right on.

"Must have been kind of lonely. Did you have close neighbors?"

"No, sir."

"Well, tell me about it, Ellsbeth. Where is this house? Who lives in it now?"

So I told him where it was and that it was vacant, and before I could stop myself I went on about the tank and the pines and all. I sort of forgot Mr. Millard was the person I was talking to, and I got carried away with homesickness for that house and the past.

114

He brought me back to the present quickly, though. "Very interesting. Ah, I see you have studies to do. Good night, Ellsbeth." And he got up and left. I thought it was the strangest attempt to make friends I'd ever heard of, though I had to admit he really seemed to try hard, as if my friendship mattered to him.

I watched him try to be B.J.'s friend, too. B.J. accepted him, though he plainly liked Mr. Beaver best. Then he found out Mr. Millard knew a lot of the stories about the Old West and the outlaw gangs, and there were several times I caught B.J. sitting spellbound while Mr. Millard recounted one wild tale after another.

That man even made friends with Little Henry and Maggie. He used to bring Little Henry lollipops when he came home from the bank, which I particularly resented because they made me think of Pa and his pet name for me. I began to feel that this smiling bank clerk was trying to take Pa's place.

He sure was around the house a lot. In fact, he never went anyplace except to the bank and, on Sundays, to church. I watched him one Sunday morning, and he was just prayerful enough, not too much so that you thought he was faking, and yet he didn't look bored or half asleep the way Uncle Jake always did. We tagged behind while he walked home with Ma.

"Wasn't that a good sermon, Mrs. James? I particularly like the text he used."

"Yes, Mr. Millard. Brother Anderson preaches well every Sunday. I know you'll enjoy worshiping with us."

"I'm sure I will."

I couldn't stand it! Pa used to come out of church letting out a sigh of relief and saying he was glad he was saved another week and could relax and enjoy himself. Ma always pretended to be horrified, and she'd tell him to hush, but most times she couldn't keep herself from grinning a little. Now here she was being pious and prim.

Ma acted different around Mr. Millard, that's for sure. And he paid her a lot of attention. They seemed to share some secret they weren't telling the rest of us, even though I was sure they didn't know each other that well. But they'd give each other a private look every once in a while even with other people around. At the dinner table I would suddenly see Ma and Mr. Millard exchanging a long look and sort of a smile. And they each watched the other without letting on. When Ma served dinner, she'd always have one eye out for what Mr. Millard was doing, how he liked the food and so on. Ma gave him privileges she would never have thought of giving the other boarders. For instance, she let him come into the sitting room at night to read the paper. And when he did, he'd always be peering over the top to see where Ma was. They didn't really ever talk much, except polite conversation, so I didn't understand what was going on. But I didn't like it.

Even Aunt Nelda thought Mr. Millard was "charming, charming." Uncle Fred chose him as a personal business advisor, not that he needed one. He'd corner Mr. Millard in the parlor and explain his latest scheme, most usually something to do with the oil fields, and Mr. Millard would act very serious and very interested.

"You see, if we just had the capital to go in there and explore, I know we'd make a fortune, Millard, a real fortune."

And Mr. Millard would stare off into space for a minute, and then he'd say, "I think you've got something there, Fred. We'll have to see about it at the bank. I'm sure we could arrange some financing."

Uncle Fred would smile, and do you know what Aunt Nelda did? Instead of ranting and raving about Dawsons having been farmers all these years and all that stuff, she'd smile sweetly and say, "Well, if Mr. Millard thinks it's a good idea."

He wasn't one to miss a trick. Each time she said that, quick as a flash, he'd say, "Please call me Joseph."

And every time Aunt Nelda would smile and say, "All right, Joseph."

Aunt Nelda may have thought he was charming,

but I kept remembering Pa and how you always knew he loved you, even when he teased about throwing you away in the swamp behind the tank. Pa wasn't much on so-called politeness, but he was always nice when he asked for something and you knew his thanks went real deep.

Ma thought all that politeness was wonderful. She told me so, talked about how nice it was to have a gentleman in the house, which I thought was unfair to our other boarders. Anyway, there was a big change in Ma almost overnight. She had more energy and she worked harder. Now she insisted she had to cook the dinner every night, as though my cooking were good enough for everyone else but not for Mr. Millard. And she took more interest in how the house looked. She was getting back to her old self again, but for all the wrong reasons.

One time I asked her, kind of sly, what had suddenly made her change. She got very proper and told me she was working hard for the boardinghouse for the sake of us children. I didn't think that was it at all. I thought it plain made Ma happy to have a man like Joseph Millard paying the same kind of attention to her that Pa used to. I'd rather have had her fainting in the parlor and letting me do all the work.

She clinched it for me the day she was in the kitchen kneading bread dough, and she stopped to look at me and said, "Ellsbeth, doesn't he remind you some of your pa?"

I didn't have to ask who "he" was. I knew. "No, ma'am," I muttered and hurried out of the kitchen.

By the time Uncle Charlie came, I was ready to explode, and my dislike for Mr. Millard had replaced any lingering resentment I might have felt for my new Aunt Annabelle.

Uncle Charlie took his bride on a sort of tour of East Texas, first to Dalton Corners to meet Grandma and Grandpa James and then down to Center to see us. Of course we didn't have room for them and they had to stay with Uncle Charlie's old landlady, but they ate at our house and spent most of their time with us.

Annabelle wasn't so bad. I expected someone with frills and curls, very ladylike. She *was* a lady in every sense of the word, but she was a real person, too. Her hair was blond, as I'd thought it would be, and piled on her head, but she fixed it in a fairly simple way without lots of curls, and she wore everyday muslins, just like the ones Ma made me wear. Best of all, she pitched in and helped with cooking and washing dishes.

I didn't realize it at the time, but Annabelle was real smart in her treatment of me. She almost but not quite ignored me. I had expected my new aunt to gush over me and predict what great friends we'd be. She never did. When we were introduced, she smiled and said Uncle Charlie had told her a lot about me and let it go at that. She seemed to understand how I felt about Uncle Charlie, and she took her sweet time making friends. In the end, she got to be as special to me as Uncle Charlie.

"Charles," she suggested one day during their short stay, "why don't you take Ellsbeth for a walk back to their old house? She's mentioned the tank and the way you used to throw rocks and all. It'd be a good chance to visit."

I held my breath until Uncle Charlie said, "That's a great idea. How about it, Ellsbeth?"

"Well," I tried not to be overanxious. "If you really want to."

"Let's. Tell your ma and let's go."

"I'll tell Lucille," Annabelle offered.

Uncle Charlie took my hand, which I was a little shy about, but we set off, arms swinging and me trying to match his great long steps.

"You walk like a boy, Ellsbeth. Been wearing pants lately?"

"No." I giggled.

"Spittin' seeds?"

"No, sir."

"How's Lavine?"

"Fine, I guess. She doesn't talk much."

"But she's around a lot?"

"She keeps me company."

"You been working pretty hard?"

"Yes."

"The boardinghouse is a success, and mostly due to you. How do you like your boarders?"

"I kind of like Mr. Beaver, and he's been specially good to B.J. Mr. Andrews keeps to himself, never even talks at dinner, so I don't know much about him. 'Course B.J. doesn't like having his schoolteacher with us, and Mr. Eastman does talk about poetry and junk at the dinner table, but he's not bad."

"You left out Mr. Millard."

"Ma really likes him. Says he's a gentleman."

Uncle Charlie's voice was dry with amusement. "I know what your ma thinks. How about you?"

"He's very polite."

"Ellsbeth!" It was a command.

"I don't know, Uncle Charlie. There's something about him. . . ."

"Now you're being truthful. I could tell something about him was bothering you." He stooped down to pick a stem of Johnson grass and put it between his teeth. "Ellsbeth, are you sure you aren't a little jealous? Mr. Millard's coming has made a big difference in your ma. She's real pleased to have him around. Isn't that what's bothering you?"

"Ma's trying to replace Pa with Mr. Millard! She

even asked me if I didn't think he looked like Pa."
I stopped dead in the road and stared at him. "Uncle
Charlie, I just couldn't stand it if someone took Pa's
place."

"Ellsbeth, my love, you're growing up before your
time. But you're right, your ma still feels lost without your pa." Uncle Charlie fell silent, then muttered under his breath, "And so do I." In a minute
he resumed the thread of his worrying. "She's got
blinders on right now, and I'm afraid she'll make
a mistake."

"What kind of mistake?" My stomach lurched at
the thought of what he was saying.

"A marrying kind." He saw the look on my face
and tried to reassure me. "Now hold on. I don't say
she'll get married right away, and I don't say Joe
Millard's the wrong man. I don't know enough
about him, except that you don't like him. He may
be fine, in spite of that. In fact, he seems nice enough.
And Lord knows, he's as taken with your ma as she
is with him. But it's just too soon for your ma to
make such a decision. She isn't thinking clearly yet.
She's got over her grief too fast and too sudden."

"Uncle Charlie, if you'd come back to Center, Ma
might listen to you—"

"I doubt that, Ellsbeth. I . . . ah. . . ." He
looked kind of funny at me. "I can't make your
ma happy the way Joe Millard does. Besides, I have
a job in Dallas and Annabelle to think about, too.

Your ma and you kids aren't my only responsibility anymore."

We had reached the old house, which now looked more dilapidated than ever. I stood in the gate and stared, feeling a sharp pang of longing for Pa and the way things used to be. That rickety old house held more happy memories than the big clean house we had now, and it brought back Pa to my mind sharply. I wanted to go back to the past so bad I almost cried. Uncle Charlie let me look for a long time; then he took my hand gently.

"Come on, Ellsbeth, let's go down to the tank."

We walked a ways, and then he suddenly let out a yell. "Race ya, and I'll give you a head start."

"I don't need a head start," I hollered, as I took off.

We arrived at the tank at almost the same time, both breathless from running and laughing.

"You run pretty fast for a girl, but I bet you can't chunk rocks as far as I can."

I picked up a good-sized one and threw as hard as I could. Then Uncle Charlie took a turn, and we had a contest that must have gone on for fifteen minutes.

With his challenges and jokes, Uncle Charlie turned our outing into a lighthearted, happy affair, but what he said about Ma wearing blinders stayed in my mind and bothered me.

And something I'd seen at the old house nagged

at a corner of my mind. There were fresh horse droppings in the yard and signs of a fire. I didn't tell
Uncle Charlie because he already thought I had too
much of an imagination, but I could see that someone had been using that house, and I knew Mr.
Wilkerson hadn't rented it out again. It gave me
an eerie feeling, kind of like that feeling that makes
people talk about someone walking on your grave.
We walked home slowly, going the long way around
the edge of town and coming up to our house from
the back, through the pine trees, so we didn't see
a soul the whole way. I was real quiet, but Uncle
Charlie must have thought it was just homesickness.
It wasn't only that. I was curious about what was
going on at that house.

Annabelle cemented our friendship in one incident just before she and Uncle Charlie left. Very
casually, she said, "Ellsbeth, I bet your hair gets in
your way in the kitchen, doesn't it?"

"Yes, ma'am. But I don't want it cut." A touch of
defiance crept into my voice.

"No, not with lovely thick hair like yours." She
dropped the subject for a while, but a little later
she came into the kitchen with a brush and a big
comb in her hand.

"Want to try something?"

"What?" I asked suspiciously.

"Brushing your hair back and fastening it out of

124

the way with this comb." I guess Annabelle knew how much I resisted anything feminine or designed to make me look like a girl, because she added quickly, "It may not look as good, but it'll keep it out of your way, and it'll be cooler in the kitchen."

"Okay."

Of course, it looked worlds better, neater and all, and I let her show me how to do it. It took some practice, and I never did get it as neat as Annabelle did, but I began wearing my hair back after that. Even B.J. noticed.

"What're you trying to do? Look like a lady?"

And Mr. Beaver said, "That looks mighty nice, little lady. Kind of grown-up, but right pretty."

I blushed and went on my way.

When Annabelle and Uncle Charlie left, B.J. and Little Henry and I went down to the train station to see them off. Ma said she had to stay home with Maggie, and somehow I thought she looked relieved to see them go. She and Uncle Charlie had had a long talk behind closed doors the night before, and Ma had looked a little uncomfortable ever since. So she kissed them both, said how glad she was they'd come, and fled into the house before we'd even reached the road.

"Here, Uncle Charlie, I'll carry that little bag."

"You will not. B.J. and I can manage the bags. You and Annabelle watch Little Henry."

At the station, Annabelle kissed each of us quickly and lightly on the forehead, promised to send B.J. a ball and bat from Dallas, and said, kind of off-handedly, that she might have some dresses for me. Uncle Charlie gave us bear hugs.

"Ellsbeth, you're up enough in school now you could write to me once in a while, you know."

"Write a letter?"

Annabelle laughed. "We'd love to hear how the boardinghouse is going and school and all."

"And there might be some other things you could keep me posted on," Uncle Charlie whispered.

I puffed with importance. "I'll try," I promised.

"What did Uncle Charlie whisper to you?" B.J. demanded on the way home.

"Nothing. It's a secret."

"Ellsbeth, please," he begged. "I'll tell Ma."

"You will not, B.J., or I'll take a switch to you." I hadn't done that since that one morning in the old house, but I guess B.J. still believed in the possibility, because the threat always quieted him. This time he muttered, "It ain't fair," kicked at a pebble in the road, and ran on ahead.

Lavine didn't like Mr. Millard either. When he came into the house, she'd get that same kind of nervous look, only not so bad, as when she spit the watermelon seed on Uncle Charlie's hat. But pretty

soon she'd say she had to go home, to cook for Isaac
or clean or something. I knew she was making it up,
because Isaac never got home till late, and one day
she said at two in the afternoon she had to start his
supper. Now I couldn't wait to tell her about my
talk with Uncle Charlie.

"But he doesn't dislike him, Ellsbeth."

"No-o . . . that's not what he said. But he's afraid
Ma wants to marry him, and I think he'd help me
stop that."

"That would be awful," she agreed.

"Lavine, why don't you like him? I mean, is it
just because I think he's a fake or because I think
Ma pays too much attention to him?"

"No, Ellsbeth, it's not any of those things . . .
it's Isaac. He . . . he made me promise not to tell."
Her voice shrank to a whisper, and she stared hard
at the ground.

"Lavine!" Her name came out as a shrill squeak,
I was so impatient to know what terrible secret Isaac
had told her.

"You promise?" Those dark eyes looked ever so
big and solemn.

"Of course, I promise, I promise. Now tell me."

If I had expected a big revelation, I was in for
a disappointment. All she said was that Isaac told
her Mr. Millard was as nice and polite as he could
be when he came into the store to discuss bank mat-

ters with Mr. Wilkerson, but when Mr. Wilkerson wasn't there, he was rude to Isaac, ordered him around, and, worst of all, cheated him out of a dollar on a purchase once.

A dollar was a whole lot of money, and I was appalled, even though I was disappointed that Lavine hadn't revealed that Mr. Millard was a thief and murderer. "Why doesn't Isaac tell Mr. Wilkerson?" To me, the solution looked simple.

"Nobody'd believe Isaac over Mr. Millard . . . and Isaac says we have to be sure not to be near any trouble if we want to stay in Center."

I began to think about what she'd told me, and the more I thought, the more sense it made. Mr. Millard was rude to Isaac and cheated him because Isaac was just a clerk, not anybody important. It showed how two-faced he was. Why was everyone else so blind?

I began to make a science out of watching Mr. Millard, but things only got worse. He took to reading to Ma at night in the sitting room, while B.J. brought in the wood and I did dishes. Ma seemed to forget that we had studies to do. She'd let us work, and she'd sit sewing and listening while he read, mostly poetry, like stuff by Browning and Tennyson and all. I listened outside the doorway a time or two, but I didn't think any of it was remarkable. And it reminded B.J. of Longfellow, whom he absolutely hated. He began to resent Mr. Millard just a little more.

Mr. Millard came to us in September. By October, Ma was calling him "Joseph," and by November, she was spending every evening listening to him read poetry. She began to ask him what his favorite foods were, and would you believe we had to eat liver and onions because "Joseph likes it"? He got fresh linen twice a week, instead of once like the other boarders, and Ma even took to ironing his shirts. As I say, there was a big change in her. She got back her energy and worked the way she used to when Pa was alive. And she was happy. She'd laugh with Mr. Millard over the silliest things, and she got so she'd talk to poor Mr. Andrews at the dinner table. She wasn't even as serious and critical as she used to be with Pa. Why, I bet if Joseph Millard had wanted to be deputy sheriff, she never would have said a word.

Of course, this wasn't all one-sided. Mr. Millard courted Ma, he really did. What else can you call reading poetry aloud at night? And he took her arm on the way home from church and did all those little considerate things that had never mattered to Pa. He honest to gosh looked happy around Ma, but he never burst out laughing the way Pa had.

I had known trouble was coming all along, but I sensed it was real close the night in December when

Mr. Millard took Ma to see the traveling opera troupe at Center's opera house. Taking her someplace was really courting, according to my definition, and I asked Ma about it.

"Ellsbeth, really! Joseph just knows that I enjoy such things, and he has kindly offered to escort me. You children will be all right, and you'll have the other boarders in case you need anything."

They left, Ma wearing her best black taffeta, the only good dress she owned and one she had had to mend and remake over the years. It looked pretty good, and she did seem awfully happy.

I was gloomy. And that night, Baby Maggie decided to throw a temper tantrum. At eight months old, she just took a crying fit for no reason. I couldn't stop her, even when I rolled her around in the wagon the way I used to do with Little Henry. Even he was upset by her crying and kept wailing, "Make her stop, 'Lsbeth. Henny sleepy." By the time I tried to comfort him and quiet Maggie and get B.J. to go on to bed, I was out of patience.

Ma was repentant when she came home. "I never should have left you," she cried, swooping up Maggie, who immediately snuggled into her arms, stopped crying, and fell asleep.

Holding that sleeping baby, Ma stood there with a rapturous look on her face and said. "Oh, Ellsbeth, it was wonderful, just wonderful. The opera is so uplifting. And Joseph is so thoughtful!"

I had to ask the question I dreaded. "Ma, you aren't going to marry Mr. Millard, are you?"

"Heavens no, Ellsbeth. But I do enjoy his company. No, though, I'll never marry again."

But that's just what she did. Ma married Joseph Millard in January the year that I was thirteen. She barely waited out the year of mourning since Pa died. Less than a month before, we'd marked the anniversary of Pa's death. Ma had worn heavy black mourning for the day and sobbed because Dalton Corners was too far for us to go visit the grave. I didn't see much sense to making a big thing of it being one year since Pa died. I knew I'd missed him fiercely every day of that long year, and this one day was no worse, no better than any other.

It came the week after Christmas, of course, which was pretty bad in itself. Everybody, including the boarders, gathered at the boardinghouse for Christmas dinner, so there was a houseful of people. I always thought lots of people at holidays meant happiness, but it didn't work that time. There was no spark, as though there was no reason to keep us in the holiday mood. I knew it was Pa we were missing, because he'd always enjoyed Christmas as much as us kids, and he'd made it better for us. Uncle Jake and Aunt Nelda and all the others just sat solemnly and thanked people for their gifts and said how good the turkey was, while all the time Ma dabbed at her eyes with her handkerchief.

Mr. Millard was as helpful as he could be, even putting up what few decorations we had. All the time he told Ma not to worry; he understood how badly she felt at this particular season. I hated to see Ma grieving again, but in a way I was almost glad, because I figured Christmas and the day Pa had died would put Ma's thoughts squarely back on Pa and make her forget any foolishness about marrying Mr. Millard. But I was wrong. She married him after all.

I came home from school one afternoon to find not Ma but Aunt Nelda bustling around the house looking important and paying no attention to Maggie, who was crying in her crib.

"Where's Ma?"

"Oh, she's gone out on a little errand. A surprise."

"Surprise? What are you fixing, Aunt Nelda, a cake?"

"Yes, Ellsbeth, a wedding cake. You just go on and take care of the baby."

My heart plummeted to my feet. "A wedding cake?"

"Well." Aunt Nelda was reluctant to share her secret, yet she couldn't stop herself. "I guess it's all right to tell you. Your ma and Mr. Millard have gone down to Brother Anderson's parish house to get married. I'm just fixing a little reception for them, just the family and the boarders. You know, a quiet party in good taste."

I was speechless. It wasn't only that Ma had gotten married but that she hadn't even told me she was going to. Here I'd been taking care of things and kind of responsible, and suddenly she treated me like a little child again, not even grown-up enough to be told her secrets. Of course, if I'd thought clearly about it, I'd have known why Ma didn't tell me. She knew how I felt about Mr. Millard's taking Pa's place.

"Well, aren't you happy for your ma? Now go get Maggie." Then raising her voice, Aunt Nelda called, "Fred, Fred! I need wood for the stove." Turning back to her cake, she muttered, "Now where could that man have gotten to? Probably off talking to that Beaver man about oil again. Fred!"

In a trance I went to soothe Maggie. She was soaking wet and a dry diaper changed her disposition completely. She settled happily in my lap as I sat in the chair rocking her and trying to sort out things in my mind. I hadn't even had a chance to call Uncle Charlie for help!

"Ellsbeth, get B.J. and you-all put on your Sunday clothes. You have to greet your new stepfather."

My only thought was that I might be sick at the idea of Mr. Millard as my stepfather. How could Ma have done that to us?

"Ellsbeth! Did you hear me?"

"Yes, ma'am." How was I going to tell B.J.? I went outside and started back toward the school. B.J., having dawdled in the school yard to play ball with his friends, met me before I got too far.

"What's the matter, Ellsbeth? You look awful!"

No use mincing words, I thought. "Ma's married Mr. Millard, and we have to go home and put our best clothes on."

My mind flashed back to Uncle Charlie running into the yard announcing that Pa had been shot. B.J. reacted the same way to my news as he had that day. He ignored it.

"Ellsbeth, I asked you what's the matter."

"And I told you."

Suddenly his voice grew distant and awed. "You meant it, didn't you?"

"Yes, B.J., I meant it."

"Oh, Ellsbeth," he wailed and grabbed my hand, a gesture totally out of character for him now that he was feeling like a grown-up nine-year-old. We were closer than we'd been since Pa died. "I wanted her to marry Mr. Beaver. Not somebody who reads poetry."

I was disgusted. B.J. had missed the point entirely. Ma shouldn't have married anyone, but most of all not Joseph Millard! Without talking, I dragged him home.

Ma and Mr. Millard arrived at the house in the late afternoon, and we four children, even little Maggie, were properly dressed in our good clothes and lined up to meet them. Ma appeared a little embarrassed and avoided looking directly at me. She fluttered over the little children instead and kept saying, "Isn't this wonderful? Mr. Millard is going to take care of all of us from now on."

I thought our new stepfather looked a little uncomfortable each time she said that, as though his new responsibilities might overwhelm him. But he never lost that big smile, I'll say that for him. Ma told each of us to step up and kiss our new stepfather, and it was an ordeal for me. I kind of put my cheek forward, and he gave me a great big kiss. If he hadn't also grabbed my hands, I'd have probably wiped my cheek. Neither B.J. nor I said a word, but Little Henry looked at him with great puzzlement and said, "Father?" Mr. Millard made some remarks about what a happy family we were going to be and what a proud man he was, and Ma just blushed.

The boarders had come in by that time and joined us for cake and some kind of watery punch that Aunt Nelda had concocted. Mr. Andrews ate his cake, shook Mr. Millard's hand, and left, while Mr. Beaver sat in a corner with Uncle Fred, telling tales from the oil fields. Mr. Eastman used the occasion to try to be chummy with B.J., asking if he wasn't glad to have a new father and wasn't this a nice surprise. B.J. dug his toe into the velvet carpet, then studied it as if it had a will of its own, and muttered, "Yessir."

I remembered what Ma had said about her wedding with Pa, and I bit my tongue to keep from asking her if anyone had sung "Oh, Promise Me" at this one. I knew even thinking it was mean.

Uncle Jake kept making loud remarks about how glad he was Mr. Millard had taken on the responsibility of our family.

"Sure is a load off my mind, Joe. Glad to have you in the family," and he slapped our new stepfather so hard on the back that he coughed and nearly choked on his cake.

"Ellsbeth," B.J. whispered, "do we have to call ourselves Millard now?"

"I don't know for sure, B.J., but I don't think so."

"I'll run away from home."

"Can I go too?" For a while, I really thought about running away. Grandpa James's farm seemed like a safe haven where I could put Ma and Mr. Millard out of my mind and I wouldn't have to work so hard. And it would serve Ma right. I even began to plan how I'd get there on the train and whether or not I'd take B.J. with me. It was a comforting dream, and I held tight to it all evening.

Maggie and I were moved up to Mr. Millard's room, and late that night I sat myself down at the table with pencil and paper and carefully wrote, "Dear Uncle Charlie, Ma got married to Mr. Millard today. Can you come home?" I had searched earlier in my secret hiding place downstairs for the piece of paper Uncle Charlie had given me with his address, and I copied it on the outside of the paper. In the morning at school I planned to glue it together so the paper itself would be the envelope. I suppose I could have asked Ma for an envelope, but she would have wondered why.

The news of Ma's marriage had spread all over town by the next morning, and all the kids at school teased me. "Got a new father, Ellsbeth!" and "Must have lots of money, huh, 'cause he works in the bank?" and, the question that hurt most of all, "What d'ya call him, Ellsbeth? Pa?"

Lavine stuck by my side like glue, silent but always there. She knew what a tragedy this was for me. When the other kids teased, she told me not to pay any attention. "There's always going to be somebody ready to poke fun at you for something," she said.

After school, Lavine and I went home by the post office so I could mail my letter.

"What will your uncle do, Ellsbeth?"

"I don't know, Lavine. I just don't know. But he's the only hope I've got." Way back in my mind, I knew Uncle Charlie couldn't do anything. And in the cold light of day, I knew I couldn't run away to Dalton Corners. Ma would probably send Uncle Jake to bring me home! I was stuck with life in the boardinghouse and with Joseph Millard. I wouldn't have thought it possible, but our lives had gone from bad to worse.

8

Ma's honeymoon was sweet enough, I suppose. But it sure was short. At first, Joseph Millard did all the little things that are supposed to make women happy; he held her chair at the dinner table and thanked her formally each night for "an excellent meal, truly excellent." He was always paying her compliments, telling her how beautiful she looked or what a good cook she was or something like that. I have to admit, it was what Ma needed. She blossomed. Whatever else was wrong with Joseph Millard, he gave Ma back a sense of herself. She could talk all she wanted about having married someone to take care of us—that's what she told us—but I knew better. Ma did it for herself.

They began to have a regular social life, more so than Ma ever did with Pa. She always was the kind who just wanted to stay home with her family, and Pa was the one who went out and had friends all over town. But they never had people come to call, and Ma never had many friends beyond ladies she knew at the sewing circle. When she was in trouble, she called Uncle Jake and Aunt Nelda, but they never came to see us otherwise, except on holidays when they felt they ought to. But now people came to call on Ma and Mr. Millard. Even Aunt Nelda and Uncle Fred came to visit. Mr. Millard was a gracious host.

"Whiskey, Fred?"

"Don't mind if I do. Thanks."

Aunt Nelda would frown ever so slightly, but Ma just looked serene. She wasn't about to cross the man who had changed her life around, especially over something so petty as a glass of whiskey. And no matter how much Aunt Nelda disapproved of the whiskey, she wanted more to be on the good side of her dashing new brother-in-law. Mr. Millard and Uncle Fred would go off to talk about money while Aunt Nelda and Ma drank chamomile tea in the parlor. Uncle Jake and Aunt Thelma came to call too, but about all Uncle Jake ever said was how glad he was Mr. Millard was looking after the family. They were out on the back stoop, but we could hear them clear in the parlor, and Ma was embarrassed. She could whisper it to me, but she didn't like anyone saying that to Mr. Millard.

One time Ma even had her ladies' sewing circle to the house for one of their regular meetings. I heard Mr. Millard urge her to do it. In fact, he nearly told her to. He said that now they had taken their part as a family in the church, he thought she ought to do her share of the entertaining. Ma had never done that before, but she was real glad to try, and as I listened to her and Mr. Millard talking about it, I realized that was another thing he'd done for Ma. Besides making her feel appreciated, he'd made her part of the life of Center in a way that not even Pa had done.

Anyway, the ladies all came and had lemonade. Ma had ordered extra ice from the icehouse, and she made dainty little cakes. They all raved over the refreshments and how well she was looking and happy and all that.

"I declare, Lucille, marriage does agree with you."

"Thank you, Mabel," she said primly.

"That Mr. Millard's a charmer, a real charmer. You're lucky to have caught him, Lucille," chimed in another woman. I guess Ma resented the idea that she had caught Mr. Millard, so she just blushed and didn't say anything.

I know he did it deliberately, but Mr. Millard said it was pure coincidence that he came home from the bank to pick up some papers he'd left by mistake. I think he just wanted to make a big impression on the ladies. He arrived while they were there; they all tittered and smiled at him, and he fussed over each one. They left thinking Ma was the luckiest woman in the world. In a way, I guess she thought so too. Anyway, she sure was happier.

Of course, I wasn't happy at all, and I avoided my stepfather whenever I could. At first, he kept on being nice to me, and there were times I was almost ashamed of myself. But a month or so after the wedding, I began to notice that he stopped trying so hard to be cordial. He still played with Little Henry and told wild stories to B.J., but he almost ignored me. I guess he figured from my attitude that friendship with me was a lost cause, and he gave up wasting his charm.

I missed Uncle Charlie pretty badly those days. He never had answered my letter, although Ma said she and Mr. Millard had gotten a letter of congratulations from him and Annabelle. I could see how Uncle Charlie would be disappointed in Ma. He probably felt just the way I did that she'd replaced Pa with Mr. Millard. But he could have written me, and I guess he would have if he knew how badly I missed him.

Everything else was all right for a couple of months, but then little things changed the atmosphere of our house. Joseph Millard seemed to be getting fidgety or bored or nervous. At the time, I thought the responsibilities of family life were getting to him.

The first incident I really remember happened early one evening. Mr. Millard—I still called him that, couldn't help myself—went into the bedroom and came right out, his charming front somewhat changed.

"Who took my wooden lockbox?"

Ma, B.J., and I stared at him kind of blankly. We didn't know what lockbox he was talking about, let alone who took it. His angry eyes landed on me first, I guess because he knew I didn't like him and he thought I'd do something mean to him.

"Ellsbeth, it was you, wasn't it?"

Well, it made me mad to be accused of something I didn't do. "No, sir, I did not. I wouldn't touch your old lockbox, whatever that is." Real defiance showed in my voice, and it only made him angrier. He forgot any idea of being charming and walked toward me, a hand raised as though he were going to whack me. I'd never been hit before in my life, except for Pa's switch, which was completely different, and my knees began to knock, no matter how much I tried to stand still and act calm. Ma must have been bothered too, for I heard her draw in her breath sharply. That was enough to remind Mr. Millard where he was, and he lowered his hand. He looked hard at Ma, as though he were trying to read her thoughts and couldn't, and then turned his head brusquely. Ma just lowered her eyes. She'd seen the ugly side of Joseph Millard, and I confess I was glad.

Little Henry had disappeared when this scene began, and I thought he had run to his bed out of fright. But he came in carrying a small wooden box, still locked, and held it up to Mr. Millard without saying a word. I was proud of his bravery, and I hoped Mr. Millard would have the sense to feel the same way.

He did. He was kind of surprised and muttered, "Thank you, Henry," and turned away, but not before he checked the box to make sure it was still locked. He had almost regained his usual charming manner, but as he headed for the bedroom, I heard him mutter, "Damn kids!" Then he slammed the door behind him, leaving us to stare at each other.

Ma finally managed to speak. "Henry? Why did you take the box?"

"Because it was locked," he said simply. "I wanted

144

to bust it open." And he pounded an imaginary box with his fist.

If it hadn't been such a revealing incident, it would have been funny. But none of us could find the heart to laugh at Little Henry.

As soon as I could, I went outside to peek in the window and find out what was in the lockbox that could be so important. Joseph Millard was sitting at the table with a bunch of papers spread out before him and a telegram in his hand. He'd read the telegram and study what looked like a calendar, and then he'd make some notes. When I took another look, I had to stop myself from letting out a long whistle. There was money, lots of it, in stacks in the box. And as I watched he began to count it, every once in a while figuring on a piece of paper. I watched for a while, in a trance, till I realized Ma would wonder where I was. I didn't tell Ma what I'd seen. I know that sounds strange, but it was like not telling Uncle Charlie about someone being at the old house. I didn't think she'd have believed me, and besides I couldn't tell her I'd been peeking. I knew spying was wrong, but I figured it was necessary in this instance. Ma would never understand that, though. She'd just see the wrong in it. I couldn't really tell anyone what I'd seen. I was going to have to watch him more closely and figure this one out myself.

The whole thing was over and forgotten by everyone else pretty soon, and our lives went on almost as normally. Mr. Millard didn't let his meanness out again, but little things began to show his disenchantment. He still listened patiently to Uncle Fred, though I thought he didn't pay quite as close attention, and he still read aloud to Ma at night. But he stopped smiling at her so much, and he rarely held her chair at the dinner table.

There were other things. He got kind of fussy about the way Ma ironed his shirts, and he'd make her do them over if they weren't just right. And he didn't like chicken-fried steak, said so right at the table in front of all the boarders after Ma had worked one night to fix it. I knew that hurt her because she must have thought about the chicken-fried steak she made the first night she cooked for him.

Ma acted more and more nervous with him, as if whatever was bothering him was her fault. If he refused to wear a shirt, she'd apologize and iron it over right then, even though I couldn't see much the matter with it. And every Sunday morning she kept trying to make polite conversation about the church service. She just didn't seem comfortable with him anymore, the way she always had with Pa, and she began to droop again, losing that newfound brightness. Annabelle had told me once that when a woman is loved, the way Uncle Charlie loved her, she gets prettier. That had happened to Ma at first, but now I thought the process was reversing itself slowly.

Of course, it wasn't that way all the time. Sometimes Mr. Millard still seemed to love Ma, or at least to like her, and he still complimented her now and then. Once he talked a long time about enlarging the boardinghouse, making it kind of a tourist home. He said we could have a really well-known place in five or ten years. I thought someone ought to tell him tourists were rarely attracted to Center.

In front of others, Mr. Millard was just the same as he always had been, charming and polite. He was apparently respected at the bank, and people thought he would turn into a pillar of the town. Brother Anderson stopped me on the street one day and told me how happy he was for Ma that she had made such a good marriage so soon after Pa's death. I couldn't blurt out that she shouldn't have married anyone, let alone Mr. Millard, so soon, and I couldn't even whisper that Mr. Millard wasn't as nice as he seemed, so I stared at the ground and said thank you.

But I was really confused that things could seem one way and really be another, or maybe it was that a person could seem one way to a lot of people and another way to Lavine and me. My mind went in circles a lot as I tried to puzzle matters out.

Lavine was no help. "He's mean, Ellsbeth. It just hasn't come out all the way yet." She said this with an air of smug certainty that indicated disaster was just around the corner for us. I hadn't even told Lavine about the money I saw the night Mr. Millard got so mad and I peeked in the window. Even so, without knowing that, she was sure something really bad was going to happen. I was almost mad at her because I believed it, and I was frightened.

"Well, Lavine, you can't just say that and then forget it. What can we do?"

Lavine was a fatalist. She saw all of us as helpless victims. "Nothing."

I refused to believe her. "I'm going to write Uncle Charlie again."

Lavine just shrugged, but I went home that afternoon and wrote another of my secret letters to Uncle Charlie. "Something bad is going to happen. Please come home. Love to Annabelle."

Not long afterward, Mr. Millard gave Lavine and me more evidence to back up our opinion of him. Isaac came to our door one night, looking very anxious.

"I'm sorry to bother you, but is Lavine here? She

isn't at home, and I was concerned about her. She's usually not out this late."

"Good gravy, no, Isaac. She's not here."

Ma came to the door to ask what was the matter, but she wasn't much help. I finally told Isaac to come inside.

"I really don't want to bother you." Isaac had big dark eyes like Lavine, and now they looked worried. She was the only person he had left in the world, and I knew Isaac really loved Lavine and tried the best he could to make her life happy. Trouble is, he wasn't given to happiness himself, coming from the same sad situation she did. He didn't even look like a happy man, tall and thin and too stooped for a young man. He was old before his time and looked as if he'd had to work too hard too soon. I felt sorry for him, and right now I was doubly sorry and worried about Lavine.

"She usually tells you where she is, doesn't she, Isaac?"

"Yes, Ellsbeth, she does. She never goes anywhere without letting me know. I just thought she might have lost track of the time and still be here. I know she spends a lot of time with you, and you've been good to her. I appreciate it."

"She doesn't come around too much lately," I muttered, and Ma picked it right up.

149

"No, we haven't seen much of her lately."

I just scowled. I knew why Lavine didn't come around.

Isaac started to edge toward the door. "I hate to cause a fuss. I'm sure she'll turn up, and I'll just go on now."

"No, you won't," I insisted. "Not until we find her."

Well, it all turned out fine in a few minutes. Lavine came to the door panting and out of breath, and before I could say anything, she blurted out, "Ellsbeth! I can't find Isaac. Where could he be?"

I nearly had to grab her and shake her so she'd be quiet and listen to me. "He's right here, looking for you. Where've you been?"

She ignored me. "Here? Where?" and she ran to her brother. It really was something to see how glad they were to find each other. You'd have thought they'd been separated years or, at least, months. I watched them enviously as they hugged and each asked if the other was all right. B.J. and I would never be like that, I thought.

The explanation was simple. Lavine had gone to the store for some last-minute things for Isaac's supper, and she'd decided to go to Wilkerson's to meet him, but she missed him and went on home. Meantime, he'd been home and couldn't find her and left. When Lavine got home and he wasn't there, yet he wasn't at Wilkerson's, she got frightened too. Luckily, our house was where they both came.

Or was it lucky? Just as all this tale was coming out, Mr. Millard called to Ma from the dining room. "Aren't we going to have any supper tonight?"

"Just a minute, Joseph," Ma called back, as she headed into the dining room to explain.

A second later we heard him bellow, "What are those sheenies doing in my house? Having a family reunion?"

I stood rooted to the spot in horror, afraid to look at Isaac and Lavine. My only thought was a hope that Ma would have the sense to remind Mr. Millard it was our house, not his. She didn't, because I heard her say softly, "They're just leaving." I didn't think Lavine and Isaac heard her, but then they didn't need to. They'd heard him.

Isaac was already out the door without a word, but Lavine held back just a minute to whisper, "It's all right, Ellsbeth. I'll see you in school tomorrow." And then she added meaningfully, "See?"

Our dinner was a silent and strained one that night.

Uncle Charlie and Annabelle came to town a few days later, and I was sure my urgent letter was what had brought them. In fact, I asked Uncle Charlie and he said of course it was why they had come and that he was sorry they couldn't come earlier when I had first written. It was days before it dawned on me that they had other reasons to be in Center. I knew Uncle Charlie spent a lot of time at the train depot, and there was a railroad-company man visiting, but I never thought much about him because I was too wrapped up in my own problems.

If I'd been less self-centered, I probably would have gotten a clue as to what was going on. I did tell Uncle Charlie I wished he'd move back to Center, and he grinned a whole lot and said, "Annabelle and I'd like that, too, Ellsbeth. We'll see, we'll see." I didn't want to hear, "We'll see," when I needed, "Yes, we'll move back," so I forgot the whole thing.

Annabelle was the one I came to first with my problems, not Uncle Charlie, however. I went to the boardinghouse where they were staying one afternoon after school. Annabelle was soft-spoken as always. She didn't act surprised to see me, and she didn't fuss. She didn't even question why I was there until we were settled in the parlor with glasses of lemonade. Then she looked straight at me and asked, "What is it, Ellsbeth?"

"Mr. Millard. What else?"

"You still don't like him?"

I blurted out all my confusion. How, I asked, could a person change, be one way before he was married and get to be another within months after the wedding?

Annabelle wasn't a whole lot of help. Sometimes, she explained, people acted their very best to get someone to marry them, and then their true character came out after they were safely married. It was just what I had thought about Mr. Millard—his true character was coming out.

"Is Uncle Charlie's true character coming out too?"

"Oh," she said softly, "that's different. Your Uncle Charlie didn't act any different before we were married. He's just as good and kind now as he was the day I met him. He's a very special person, Ellsbeth."

I knew that, but I didn't see how you were supposed to know before you got married if the man was very special or if his true character was going to come out afterward. I might be like Ma and make a mistake, so I privately resolved not to try marriage when I got older.

We heard Uncle Charlie just then, and I remembered that he had thought I was jealous of Mr. Millard. I quickly changed the subject.

"How long are you going to stay in Center, Aunt Annabelle?"

"It depends on Charles. Let's ask him." Then she called out, "Charles? Ellsbeth and I are in the parlor."

"Ah," he said, sweeping theatrically into the room, "my two favorite ladies!"

I blushed a little but Annabelle just laughed

happily and asked, "Don't you have an announcement for Ellsbeth?"

Finger to his forehead, he pretended to think. "Let me see. Ah yes, I know." Uncle Charlie paused and stared at me while I fidgeted with curiosity. Finally he said, "That's it! I can run faster than she can."

Annabelle laughed, and I squirmed more. "What is it, Uncle Charlie? Really?"

He stared at me a minute, then grinned. "How about if I told you Annabelle and I are moving back to Center? I've been offered the stationmaster's job here, and I've decided to accept it."

I squealed with delight, forgot all my shyness, and hurled myself at him. "That's wonderful!" Uncle Charlie and Annabelle were coming back to Center! Now Uncle Charlie would see the truth about Mr. Millard! I floated home on happiness that afternoon.

When I arrived, though, I found Ma in the sitting room, crying softly into a handkerchief. I felt sorry for her, instead of being angry as I was most of the time, and I went over to put my arm around her shoulder.

"Ellsbeth," she sobbed. "It's not at all the way I thought it was going to be. I think I've made things worse for us."

Now *that* I could agree with. "Yes, Ma, I kind of think so too. But what happened?"

154

She put the handkerchief to her mouth and kind of mumbled around it. "When Joseph came home at noon, he . . . he . . . oh, it doesn't matter. It was just awful!"

"Tell me what happened, Ma." We had almost changed roles. I felt like the grown-up, prying a story out of a reluctant child.

Between sobs, Ma told me. He'd come in, being his charming self, and after lunch he'd said he needed to talk to her about something that they should have discussed long ago. It was the deed to the boarding-house.

"Now that we're married," he told her, "you'd best sign the house over to me. Legal protection and all. It's better to have it in a man's name."

Well, of course, Ma had to tell him we rented the house, didn't own it, and he flew into a rage. Ma sobbed again as she told me.

"And . . . I just know it . . . I've suspected lately. He doesn't love me!"

For the first time I dared to ask the question that had been bothering me. "Ma, do you love him like Pa?"

She stared into space a long time before she answered me. Finally, kind of low, she said, "No, Ellsbeth, I guess I don't. But I thought I did. God help me, I thought I did."

"Ma? Didn't you tell him we rented the house?"

She shook her head. "I didn't . . . well, why should I have?"

"Oh, Ma!" was all I could say. She looked so miserable that I guess she knew she'd been caught at her own game. "Did you ever talk to him about money?"

"Not much. Oh, he knows what the boarders pay, and he expects me to run the house on that. He hasn't ever given me any money . . . and I, well, I just hated to bring it up."

My joy over Annabelle and Uncle Charlie had faded, and I hadn't even told Ma their news. Instead, I stood there thinking about Mr. Millard and the money I'd seen. Greed surely was part of his character. But why did he hide all that money from Ma? And what would he have done with the deed to the house? And, most of all, I wondered how long our lives were going to go on like this.

Our life did go on the same way for quite a spell. Uncle Charlie and Annabelle were settled in Center within a month, in a little house across town not too far from our old house. But they neither one came to visit much, because it was uncomfortable when they did, and I didn't have time to go see them very often. Still, it was nice to know they were there. And one time I did manage to have a talk with Uncle Charlie. But he was like Annabelle. There wasn't much he could do.

He listened to my recital of all the bad things Mr. Millard had done—cheating Isaac out of a dollar and asking Ma for the deed to the house and yelling at me about the lockbox. But I didn't tell him about the money in the box. I had a growing feeling that the money was part of something so bad that I didn't want to know about it. People didn't hide that much money if they'd come by it honestly. But if Mr. Millard really was a robber, the kind that stole lots of money instead of just cheating Isaac out of a dollar, what would that mean to us? What would he do to us? All of a sudden, instead of wanting Uncle Charlie to do something, I was hiding the one piece of information that he probably would have taken as a cause to act.

As it was, he didn't act the least bit surprised by anything I told him. He just kind of nodded and said, "Hmmm, I see . . ." a couple of times.

Then he put his arm around me. "Ellsbeth, I've owed you an apology for a while now. You weren't just jealous. You saw something in Millard that the rest of us missed."

"But, Uncle Charlie," I begged, "can't we do something?"

"Not one sweet thing, Ellsbeth. As they say, your ma has made her own bed."

"It's not right."

"In a way it is, honey. Your ma made a decision,

and she's the one that has to live with the consequences. And no one but her can do anything about it. The only thing that isn't right is that you children have to live with her mistake."

"Are you calling Mr. Millard Ma's mistake?"

He grinned. "I guess I am."

"Ma said one time there was nothing we could do about it. We just have to go along. But I don't want to live like this for another five years till I'm grown enough to be on my own."

"What else can you do, Ellsbeth?"

"Couldn't I live with you and Annabelle?"

"And leave B.J. and Henry and Maggie? Not to mention your ma? Ellsbeth, my sweet, we'd love to have you, but it wouldn't work. You know that."

"Yeah," I muttered. I did know that.

Uncle Charlie hadn't given me any hope, but it was some comfort just to have him so close.

One night not much afterward, Ma and Mr. Millard argued pretty hard. I listened at the door, not just out of curiosity but because I figured I should keep up with Mr. Millard's doings. It was one of those senseless arguments that start over something small and end up covering everything. What sparked this argument was that the supper had been too sparse, salad and vegetables but no meat.

Mr. Millard, of course, didn't pay rent, and now I

knew he didn't pay Ma any household allowance or anything, so she had more people to feed and less money to do it on. This week she had plain run out of money. He hollered about women who didn't know how to run a household and spent money like water and so on.

"A fool. That's what I was. Taken in like a plain fool."

Softly Ma asked, "Why did you marry me, Joseph? Because you thought I owned this house?"

He laughed, an ugly, derisive chuckle. "I wish it were that simple. I could write it off as a bad business deal. But no . . . I . . . I. . . ." All at once he was at a loss for words.

"Yes?" Ma prodded.

"I thought . . . things would change."

"Change?"

"Yeah, I really had great hopes . . . but they fell through. And your four children didn't help."

For once, Ma got mad enough to raise her voice. "You leave my children out of this."

"I can't. They're part of the problem. They're always around. A man has no privacy, no freedom, no . . . oh, never mind. It wouldn't have worked anyway."

Ma was kind of desperate now. "Joseph, we're married. It's got to work. What else can we do?"

He chuckled again, and outside the door at my

listening post I winced at the sound. "We'll see. Meantime, I expect meat for dinner."

I had the feeling he'd come out the door any minute, so I crept upstairs to my room.

Mr. Beaver stood at the top of the stairs, and I guess he'd been silently watching me. He reached out and put an arm around my shoulders.

"Little miss, some people sure do hide their true colors. It's like those flowers that look so pretty and are really deadly poison. What do they call them? Oleander!"

And he went downstairs and outside for a night walk, leaving me a little consoled because someone else understood. But the thought that we were doomed to spend the rest of our lives like this was unbearable.

9

The situation came to a most unexpected head one morning late in June when B.J. had gone fishing, which he did almost every morning when school was out, and Ma sent me to the store. As I left, she was playing with Maggie out in the shade of the big hackberry tree in front of our house. It wasn't a good climbing tree, like the live oak in front of our old house, but it was a wonderful tall tree that made lots of shade.

I whistled and skipped my way to the grocery,

glad to be free of the house for a while, got Ma's groceries, and hauled them home in the wagon I'd pulled with me. I carried the first sack into the kitchen and called out, "Ma, I'm back," but there was no answer. I called again, and finally from the sitting room I heard a faint voice.

"In here, Ellsbeth."

Ma was standing rigid in the middle of the sitting room, a wadded-up handkerchief in her hand. Her eyes were red from crying, but when I burst into the room, she was dry-eyed and looked directly at me.

"Maggie's gone." She spoke in a flat, dry tone that I'd never heard her use. I froze where I stood.

"Gone?"

"Gone. Kidnapped."

"Kidnapped? By Gypsies?" Somehow I crossed the room to her. She grabbed me and held tight.

"No, Ellsbeth, not Gypsies." She paused as if she could hardly get the words out. "By Joseph Millard."

I couldn't believe it. Why would Mr. Millard kidnap Maggie?

Before I could ask Ma, she cried out, "Ellsbeth, I'm afraid." Tears began to roll down her cheeks, but she didn't sob aloud.

"Ma, don't, please." I was desperate, afraid for Maggie, hurting for Ma, and still so confused I didn't know what to do. "Ma, I'll go get Sheriff Green."

"No!" She screamed at me so loud I jumped.

Then she spoke more softly. "No, Ellsbeth, you mustn't. That would make him hurt Maggie, even —" She broke into a loud sob.

"Ma, please tell me what happened."

Slowly she began to tell the story, her voice a weird mixture of anger and fright with a touch of steely hatred every time she mentioned Mr. Millard. It seems he had rushed home in the middle of the morning, burst into the house, and announced he was leaving town immediately. He was as calm as could be, and he told Ma she had to come with him for safety. Ma didn't understand and said so, and he told her she was a fool, but that no one would touch him if she was with him. Ma thought he'd gone crazy and told him she wouldn't go, but just then, she said, he acted as if he had a new idea and said he'd take Maggie instead. She'd keep him safe.

Ma pleaded then and said that he couldn't take her baby, but he pulled a gun! It was a tiny derringer, Ma said, but he held it steady and told her to keep out of his way or he'd shoot. Then he grabbed his precious wooden lockbox, took the baby, and left. He kind of said good-bye to Ma and something about it being nice while it lasted, but the last thing he told her, in a cold voice, was that if she ever wanted to see Maggie again, she'd better not go near the sheriff. At the end of her story Ma collapsed into sobs again.

I never had heard anything like it, and I agreed

with Ma that Mr. Millard was dangerous. Of course, Lavine and I'd thought so all along, but knowing it was true wasn't going to help get Maggie back. I was trying to figure out what to do when I heard a knock on the door and a man's voice.

"Mrs. Millard . . . uh . . . Lucille?" It was Sheriff Green, and I didn't care what Ma thought about calling him, I was awfully glad to see him.

He came into the room looking kind of embarrassed but also looking around as if he expected someone to jump out of a corner at him. I noticed one hand was on his gun the whole time, even though he managed to use the other to tip his hat politely at Ma.

"Ma'am . . . uh . . . I have to ask where your husband is."

"He's gone," she said in that flat voice.

"Gone," I told the sheriff, "and taken the baby with him. He told Ma not to tell you if she ever wanted to see Maggie again."

Ma drew her breath in real sharp, just as she had when Mr. Millard almost hit me, but she didn't say anything. Just nodded her head to testify to the truth of what I was saying.

The sheriff exploded. "Took the baby with him! Why that dirty. . . ." I guess he remembered where he was because he didn't finish the sentence.

"Sheriff," I asked, "what's going on? Ma says Mr.

164

Millard rushed in here this morning and pulled a gun on her. I think you should arrest him."

I guess I sounded pretty self-righteous, because in spite of how serious things were, the sheriff grinned just a little. "Ellsbeth, that's just what I'd like to do if I could find him."

"You would? You knew he kidnapped Maggie?"

"No, I want him for"—he glanced at Ma as if he wasn't sure he should say it, then took a deep breath and went on—"bank robbing."

"The money! That's it!" I spoke without thinking, but Sheriff Green picked it right up.

"What money, Ellsbeth?"

"Ah . . ." I hemmed and hawed but finally had to admit that I'd peeked in at Mr. Millard, and I had to tell them about the stack of money that had been worrying me so. My worst expectations had come to pass.

Ma just gasped and put her hand over her mouth, and finally, in a horrified tone, she said, "A bank robber!"

The words carried out the door to B.J., who was just coming up the walk to the house.

"Who's a bank robber?" He rushed into the room, his face all lit up with the hope of excitement.

"Hush, B.J., this is serious."

"Who's a bank robber?" He repeated it, ignoring me.

"Your stepfather, son," Sheriff Green told him.

B.J. acted for a minute as if he didn't know who his stepfather was, then he was as unbelieving as I was. "Mr. Millard? You're crazy."

"B.J., that's no way to talk to the sheriff."

Ma turned to the sheriff, the man she'd known all her life and the man Pa had worked for. I knew Ma really hurt inside. She'd been married to a man of honor, a man who stood up for what he believed was right and fair, even when it cost him his life, and now she was married to a bank robber. I think Pa or the thought of him gave her courage. Anyway, I was surprised at her and proud. If I'd stopped to think, I'd have expected her to turn helpless again, the way she did the day Pa was shot. But the things Mr. Millard had done—fooling Ma and kidnapping Maggie—were so horrible that they must have shocked her back to her old self, like throwing cold water on a hysterical person. Now she was strong, as she used to be before Joseph Millard, before, when Pa was with us. When she spoke, her voice was calm and firm.

"Tell me about it, Luke."

So Sheriff Green shuffled his feet and told the story, haltingly, as if it saddened him too to see Ma married to such a man and made him feel guilty for having to tell her.

"Seems, Lucille, he's part of a gang. He's the real

leader, the one who plans things. He gets a job in a bank, establishes a good reputation, and gains the confidence of the people he works with until they give him a key and let him stay late by himself. Do you know whether he had any letters of reference when he came to Center?"

Ma shook her head. "No, I just assumed he had good references. He told me about coming from a bank in Colorado City and all, how he left because the bank-owner's son was jealous of his position, and all that."

"Yeah. Apparently he always tells such a good story about where he's been and why he left that no one thinks to check the letters of reference. Well, gosh, Lucille, you know how convincing he can be."

Ma nodded grimly, and Sheriff Green looked a little apologetic, but he went right on with his story.

"Anyway, he puts up a good story of working late at the bank. Then one night he lets these other fellows in and they clean out the bank. . . . There's two of them. Millard says he was held up, couldn't do anything else if he wanted to save his life."

All of us looked at the Sheriff incredulously, but there was still more.

"After a little while, he moves on, says he can't stand the memory of the robbery, feels he let the town down. Acts like a real martyr. 'Course what happens is that he goes somewhere and gets his share of the money. They've done this five, six times, and I just heard about it. Law people out in West Texas been looking for two robbers for a long while now but not Millard. Anyway, they caught one of the others out there for rustling, and rather than answer to that, he spilled all he knew about the bank robberies and Millard. He said they were planning to rob the bank in Center in about another month."

"How did Mr. Millard know they'd caught one of the men?" My mind was leaping, trying to find holes in this incredible story.

"They tell me down to the bank he got a telegram this morning. Afterward he said he had to take care of something and left." He paused a minute, then looked at Ma again.

"Uh, Lucille, did he have any extra money to spend lately? They've done a quick check of the books, and he's already embezzled some funds . . . just within the last month. Funny thing. For a long time he seems to have behaved himself."

I remembered the argument Ma and Mr. Millard had that night, and I almost answered for Ma. But she did fine herself.

"No, Luke, he didn't, he surely didn't. He must've been putting it all in that wooden box." There was no missing the bitter note in her voice, and I knew she remembered that same argument all too well.

B.J. muttered, "He don't look right or act right for a real bank robber—"

168

"Hush, B.J." I was too worried to be really impatient with B.J.'s dreams of the Old West, but Ma paid him more attention.

"You're right, B.J. He didn't look or act like a bank robber. He . . . oh, I don't know . . . he's been so different lately. But at first, I thought, I really thought—" She seemed to draw herself together again. "It doesn't matter now. We've got to get Maggie back."

"Now don't you worry. We'll get her back safe, Lucille."

"How?" Ma was back to reality. "Luke, I'm afraid he'll harm her if he's cornered. I never saw anybody act so cold and cruel as he did this morning."

"Well, of course, we'll have to find him first. I don't suppose you have any idea where he might have gone."

"None," Ma said, sounding discouraged.

Just then Little Henry wandered into the sitting room whining, "Maggie gone, Maggie gone." I shushed him and sat down with him on my lap. Ma paced back and forth in a great circle, her hands behind her back and her head bowed, and Little Henry and I sat there watching her, helpless and confused. Sheriff Green stood in a corner, shifting his hat from one hand to the other.

And that's how Uncle Charlie found us. His voice boomed out, "Lucille? Where are you?" as he came through the front door, and Ma barely had time to call, "In the sitting room, Charles," before he came striding into the room.

Ma was still calm, though I expected her to throw herself into Uncle Charlie's comforting arms. She just stood there and said, "Charles, something awful—"

"I know, I know. Just came from the bank. Word's all over town they're looking for Millard."

Ma nodded, silent a minute, then went on. "That's not all. He . . . he kidnapped Maggie."

Uncle Charlie got the grimmest look on his face I've ever seen. I sure was glad I wasn't Mr. Millard because if he had been there right then, Uncle Charlie wouldn't have hesitated to kill him, I'm sure. The only thing he said was a long, low "Oh, my God!"

I wasn't used to hearing Uncle Charlie or anyone else take the name of the Lord in vain, and his exclamation emphasized how awful the situation was.

Uncle Charlie turned to the Sheriff. "Luke, I brought this." He held out a piece of paper. "It's a copy of the telegram Millard got this morning. I can't make heads or tails out of it, though."

"Let's see," the Sheriff said, as he reached for it. "Says 'The old man is sick. Going to light the fires at the old homestead.'" He paused and stared at it as though a second reading would give meaning to the message.

"Obviously a code," Uncle Charlie said, which I

thought was pretty smart of him. "But what does it mean?"

"Beats me." Sheriff Green stuck the paper in his pocket. I guess he decided it wasn't going to help them at all.

"What are you going to do, Luke?" Uncle Charlie asked. "I'll ride with you, do whatever you think."

"Well, Charlie, I ain't so sure that's the way to do this thing. You see, he might hurt that baby. In a way, he was pretty smart taking her for protection. . . ."

While the two of them talked about the way to get Mr. Millard and B.J. hung on their every word, I sat and thought about Pa. For some reason, I kept wondering what he'd do, and I'd have to pull myself up sharp to remember that if he were here, none of this would be taking place. There never would have been a Mr. Millard in our lives. Once I caught myself almost accusing him, thinking, "Pa, how could you let this happen to us?" But I straightened up pretty quick and realized Pa himself would be more distressed than even Uncle Charlie.

Suddenly I knew where Mr. Millard had taken Maggie, and I knew I had to get her. I knew what old homestead the telegram meant. I knew as sure as shooting where they were. Sheriff Green was right, too. Mr. Millard would hurt Maggie if the men went after him. I had to go myself.

Very carefully I put Little Henry down and edged out of the room, watching closely to make sure no one noticed me. Ma and Uncle Charlie and the Sheriff and B.J. were all wrapped up in posse talk and plans for getting Maggie back. No one saw me go.

I eased out the kitchen door, then ran as fast as I could, straight for our old house by the stock tank.

I stopped running long before I got to the house, partly because I was out of breath but more because I knew I had to have a plan. I couldn't just run right up to the door and ask Mr. Millard to hand me the baby.

Our old house wasn't easy to sneak up on. It sat on the side of the road with no bushes or anything around it, just that live oak tree in front. I was pretty sure Mr. Millard had gone the back way, around the edge of town rather than through the middle where everybody would have wondered where he was going with Maggie. He could have headed out through that stand of pine behind the boardinghouse and made it all the way to the stock tank without seeing anyone. But now he surely was watching out the window toward town, and if I walked down the road, he'd see me. I studied the whole thing in my mind and decided to cut behind the row of trees across the road from the house, go past the house, and approach it from the other side.

Mr. Millard wouldn't think to watch back toward the tank and woods. I thought it was a swell plan.

As I crept along behind those trees, I sure did wish I had a plain muslin dress on instead of Annabelle's hand-me-down yellow calico. Wearing it was like waving a flag at him. And I wished even harder that I'd had the sense to stop for my shoes. Cockleburs stuck into my feet, and I knew Ma would skin me alive for crawling through bushes and behind trees in my bare feet. But then Ma'd have skinned me anyway if she knew what I was doing.

I crept back up to the window of the sitting room without seeing any sign of Mr. Millard. It was the same window B.J. and I had peeked in way back when Pa was shot, and we'd seen Uncle Charlie holding Little Henry and Ma looking so funny in the rocker.

Now the room was empty and so dark that for a minute I didn't see anything. Then I had to hold my breath to keep quiet. Maggie was in there, sitting on that dirty old floor that hadn't been swept in heaven knows how long. She looked okay, but every once in a while she kind of whimpered. I didn't see Mr. Millard at all. Where could he have gone? Surely he wouldn't have left Maggie alone in the house . . . or would he? I decided I'd just have to go in and get her.

That's when it happened. I turned around and

headed for the back door only to find myself looking straight at Joseph Millard, my stepfather. He stood real still, as if he'd been watching me for a minute or so, and he had a kind of funny half smile on his face. But he didn't look the same as usual. His clothes weren't as neat, in fact his pants were downright crumpled, and his always shiny shoes were dusty. But the thing in his hand was what made me catch my breath. He held the derringer that Ma had described.

"Good morning, Ellsbeth. Nice of you to come help me take care of Maggie." He spoke in a funny tone, as though we both knew he didn't really mean what he said.

"I . . . I . . ." All I could do was stammer.

"Get in the house." He waved the gun toward the back door, and I obeyed. As I went into the kitchen, I couldn't help thinking of all the times I'd gone in and out of that door and all the happy memories the house held. Now here I was, being followed by a man with a gun. I wanted Ma and Uncle Charlie and B.J. and Little Henry and . . . my own bed at home!

Maggie was all dirty from sitting on the floor, and she needed a change badly, but of course there wasn't anything in the house to use. The only thing in the room was that wooden lockbox on the floor. I stared at it for a minute but then turned my attention back to Maggie. Turning my back to Mr. Millard, I slipped my petticoat out from under my dress so I could rip off a corner for a washcloth and use the rest to give Maggie a dry outfit. On this hot June morning, she didn't need clothes, which was fortunate since hers were soaked and caked with wet dirt. I had to ask if I could go to the kitchen for water, and he followed me there and back with Maggie toddling along with us. I washed Maggie as best I could, which wasn't much.

Mr. Millard watched me silently all the while, still holding that derringer, and I stole a look at him every now and then. He'd lost all his charm. In fact, if Ma had met him first right then, I bet she wouldn't have looked twice. He was just a desperate, halfway frightened man.

Once I'd cleaned her up, Maggie was fine. Mr. Millard had been her friend for a while now, and this morning he'd done the best he could to be kind to her, so she wasn't frightened the way I was. But she was delighted to see me and didn't want to let go. That was all right since I didn't want her walking around in the dirt again anyway. So I sat on the floor, in one corner, with my back propped against the wall and held Maggie. Soon she went sound asleep in my arms.

Mr. Millard was restless, pacing around the room, every once in a while turning his back to me. I calculated what with holding the baby I didn't have time to run or attack him from behind or anything. He was safe to turn away from me a little bit.

Once he stopped walking and came and stood real close to me. I looked at the floor to avoid him, but he reached out to kick my foot and make me look up at him.

"Sheriff been to the house yet?" His voice was rough, not all smooth the way it always had been at home.

I figured I could ignore him and refuse to talk, which was what I really wanted to do, or I could get him talking and maybe off his guard. That seemed smarter.

"Yessir. Sheriff was there when I left."

He turned away, kind of talking to himself. "Good. He'll be slow to come after me 'cause of Maggie . . . and now you, Ellsbeth." Then he whirled to face me again. "How did you know where I was?"

I didn't figure there was any harm in telling him the truth. " 'Cause of the night you asked so much about this house . . . and then I saw horse droppings out here one day. Knew somebody'd been here."

He grinned a little. "Pretty smart, Ellsbeth. Yeah, somebody was out here. Perkins and I used this house as a meeting place." He'd been ever so slightly amused by my guess, but then he turned angry and mean again. "Who'd you tell where you were going? That uncle of yours?"

"No, sir, nobody."

"Are you sure?" He took a menacing step closer to me.

"Yeah, I'm sure," I muttered, wishing I had told Uncle Charlie about seeing the horse droppings instead of worrying that he'd laugh.

Impatient, Mr. Millard turned to the window again. "Damn! Where can Perkins be with those horses? Doesn't he know people in these parts are liable to be rope happy about bank robbers and kidnappers?" He looked back at us in disgust.

Here I thought he'd be watching the road to town and all the time he was looking out toward the stock tank, waiting for someone named Perkins to meet him. No wonder he saw me coming. I guessed Perkins must be the other member of the gang.

We must've sat like that at least an hour, me holding sleeping Maggie and Mr. Millard pacing around, looking out that back window, cursing Perkins for being late, damning Ma for ruining his plans, and occasionally bragging to me about what a smart bank robber he was.

"Made a killing. Got it with me." He walked over and stood looking at the wooden lockbox. "This is going to keep me comfortable for a long while."

I gulped. Why hadn't I told anybody about the money or the horse droppings? As I sat there scolding myself for letting fear and pride get in the way of telling Uncle Charlie all I knew and suspected, Joseph Millard began pacing and talking again.

"No one would ever have guessed, respectable member of the community that I was. And marrying your ma was the icing on the cake . . . but I shouldn't have done it." He paced again, now talking more to himself than to me. "Stupid mistake. Don't know why I thought I'd be happy living like any other man. She made it all seem possible for a while." He banged a fist into the windowsill in anger.

I never said anything, but I was beginning to figure things out. He'd thought of reforming when he married Ma! I was awestruck that she would have that much influence over a hardened criminal, but I was also pretty much awestruck at what a bad choice she'd made in men.

Finally we heard a noise out back, ever so slight, and Millard looked out the window. He muttered, "It's about time," and I knew Perkins, whoever he was, had arrived. I wondered what that meant for Maggie and me, and I was pretty sure it wasn't good.

The back door was cautiously opened, then tentative steps sounded across the kitchen, and a real soft voice called "Lee?"

I just stared at my stepfather. His name was Lee! Lee what, or was that his last name? I should have known it wouldn't be Millard. While I was pondering that, the other bank robber came into the room.

Now this one looked more like a bank robber. B.J. would have been pleased. He had on dirty Levis, dust covered from a long ride, a plaid shirt with a red kerchief, and a well-worn Stetson. His dark hair hung in long strings that looked dirty to me, and his face was covered with a stubble of beard. He nodded at Millard before he saw us, then let out an indignant yelp.

"What the hell are they doing here?"

"Hostages. To insure our freedom."

Hostages! That was the word I'd been trying to think of, and it was what Maggie and I were. I closed my eyes and prayed, "Please God, let Uncle Charlie come and get us, and I'll never complain about doing dishes or having to watch the babies or anything. Just let Uncle Charlie come."

"Got my telegram, huh?"

"Yeah," Millard replied, "nobody knew what the homestead was except Ellsbeth here, my . . . ah . . . stepdaughter."

"Stepdaughter?" Perkins yelped again. "Does that mean you got a wife too?"

Mr. Millard's reply was grim. "I sure do."

Perkins did the wrong thing. He started to laugh. "You? Married? What happened?"

Mr. Millard didn't think it was one bit funny,

and he started for Perkins with meanness in his eye. Perkins saw him and ducked just in time to avoid a hard punch. He sidled across the room, all the laughter gone.

"Okay. Sorry. It ain't so funny after all."

Mr. Millard backed off too. I guess they knew it wouldn't do them any good to fight with each other. But Mr. Millard's voice was almost sad when he went on and told Perkins about Ma.

"Ellsbeth's mother runs a boardinghouse in town. She was widowed some time ago . . . and she's a charming lady. I . . . I was a real respectable member of the community. Thought about staying that way."

Perkins didn't laugh again, but he was incredulous. "You did?"

"Yeah . . . thought I could do it. But it was part the money . . . and part"—he looked at Maggie and me again—"part family life. It, uh, didn't turn out to be what I thought."

Perkins hooted, and Mr. Millard glowered at him.

Suddenly Mr. Millard looked alarmed. "We've been standing here like dummies in the middle of the house, not watching either way. A whole posse could have snuck up on us."

I thought it was unlikely but I hoped. They walked to the windows ever so cautiously and stood on the side to peer out for what seemed like a long

180

time. Finally they decided there was no one outside.

"Looks okay. Let's get out of here." Perkins looked nervous now, as though he'd been reminded that the law was after them. "Whole town's probably after you, 'cause of them." He jerked his head in our direction.

"Yeah. I don't know what to do about them." Millard looked at us again.

"No choice. We'll have to take them with us." Perkins glanced at us again. "Pretty little baby. Too bad."

That didn't sound as if we had any hope at all. I shifted around nervously on the floor, and Mr. Millard ordered me to sit still and shut up. I hadn't said anything anyway.

He stood staring at us. "I almost hate to do that to their ma. But you're right. We'll take 'em . . . for a while anyway."

The implication of his last words frightened me beyond belief, and I sat there frozen.

Perkins got practical. "Horses are in back. I brought you a good one. We'll each have to take one kid."

Scared to death as I was, I almost said, "Dibs on not riding with Mr. Millard," but I kept my mouth shut.

"Get up, Ellsbeth." There was no politeness in Mr. Millard's voice, just a stern command. Maggie stirred and began to cry when I moved. I comforted her the best I could, but I was barely able to stand because my feet were asleep from sitting so long and my knees were knocking with fright. We finally got going, me carrying the baby, Millard leading the way, and Perkins behind us, all headed for the back door. I could tell neither Perkins nor Mr. Millard was going to feel sentimental about us and let us go home, and apparently Uncle Charlie wasn't going to make it in time to help me. If Maggie and I were going to get away, I'd have to do something myself.

And I did it. Mr. Millard forgot all his polite manners and barged through the back door first, with me right behind him. I reached out my foot, hooked it under his, and used my free hand to shove as hard as I could. Joseph Millard lost his balance, went flying out the door, rolled down the stairs of the stoop, and landed in a heap in the dry dirt at the bottom, his clothes more disheveled than ever, his composure lost.

Trouble was, I had acted on the spur of the moment, and I hadn't thought about what to do with Perkins behind me. Luckily, I didn't have to. Just as Perkins started to yell "Hey!" and grab me, a man's voice said, "Morning, Millard. Don't move. I've got a gun on you."

It *was* Uncle Charlie! He was standing right by the back steps, staring down at Millard and barely able to keep from grinning at the funny sight my formerly dashing stepfather made in the dirt.

The Perkins fellow wasn't as quick a thinker as Mr. Millard. Instead of grabbing me as he should have done if he were smart, he just turned and bolted for the front door.

"Uncle Charlie, the other one! He's going out the front door."

Calm as could be, Uncle Charlie said, "No, he won't. Sheriff Green's at the front door. Are you all right, Ellsbeth? And Maggie?"

I wanted to throw myself at him with relief, but I knew it was more important that he hold the gun, so I simply nodded and told him yes. "But I sure am glad to see you. How'd you know where he'd taken Maggie?"

"Same way you did, honey. It just took me longer to figure it out. I saw signs out here that day you and I came visiting, signs somebody'd been around, but I didn't mention it to you because I thought it would upset you."

Uncle Charlie had known all along. He wouldn't have thought I was silly! I could have kicked myself for not talking to him about what I'd seen. If I had, the whole Mr. Millard problem might have been untangled more easily and sooner.

"We've been out here a little while, Ellsbeth," Uncle Charlie went on, "but there wasn't any way

I could let you know we were around, and it wouldn't have been safe to barge in there and try to rescue you."

Turned out Uncle Charlie and Sheriff Green had three other men with them, kind of a posse, I guess. They'd left their horses clear down the road, almost to town, and come up to the house on foot.

They must have snuck up when Perkins and Mr. Millard were having that set-to about Millard's marriage to Ma! I should have known all along Uncle Charlie would take care of us, just as he promised Pa.

Sheriff Green came around the house, occasionally poking his pistol into Perkins, who shuffled in front of him. The other three men came in from wherever they'd been hiding. Uncle Charlie and Sheriff Green held the guns while one man tied up Perkins and Mr. Millard, and then the other two went after their horses and the two Perkins had brought.

You should have seen the sight all of us made coming back into town! Perkins and Mr. Millard were both tied on their horses, Mr. Millard looking a mess because of all the dirt on his clothes and because he hung his head way down to avoid seeing anyone. That was the end of his respectability. Sheriff Green led the horse with Perkins, and Uncle Charlie the other one, and Maggie and I both nestled in front of Uncle Charlie on his horse. It was the most comfortable, safe place I could imagine, and I snuggled down happily after having turned once to giggle at the sight Mr. Millard made.

Seems like the whole town was out watching as we rode down Main Street. By then I guess everyone knew about the robbers and the kidnapping. I saw Mr. Wilkerson and Florence's father, and Mr. Beaver was there, shaking his fist in Mr. Millard's direction. Next to him stood Uncle Fred, staring in disbelief. I felt kind of sad for him that he'd lost the one person who even pretended to listen to him. Way back, close to Wilkerson's store, I think I saw Lavine, looking very solemn. But I was most aware of how angry all the men of Center were. People get double mad when they are fooled, and Mr. Millard had fooled them, pretending to be a solid citizen and really meaning to take their money. And then he'd kidnapped a baby! I expect some would have lynched him right there, but they respected Sheriff Green and let him do his job.

Uncle Charlie talked to the Sheriff for a minute, then turned his horse toward our house, saying Ma was worried near to death. We rode in silence.

Ma rushed out to meet us and fussed over Maggie and me. Were we all right? Had he hurt us? But she was the old Ma. The minute she was sure we were all right, she lit into me for having taken off alone. It was a good scolding, such as I hadn't had in a year and a half, and I almost enjoyed sitting there and taking it. But a corner of my mind kept repeating that Ma had gotten us into this mess.

Uncle Charlie finally had to tell Ma to be quiet and take us in the house. Inside, I found Uncle Jake and Aunt Nelda waiting, too, and everybody talking at once.

"Just a shame what these girls have been through," said Aunt Nelda with a sniff. "Lucille, I don't know how you could bring a man like that into your house."

And Uncle Jake, "Never liked him. Never! Knew there was something funny about him."

Ma made me proud then, and I almost forgave her. "Hush, both of you. You were all in favor of my marriage to Joseph Millard, and you were as wrong as I was. Now what matters is that he's behind bars, and the girls are safe."

Everyone was talking at once about what had happened, who Joseph Millard really was, how brave I'd been, how foolish I'd been, and what next?

Uncle Jake had one opinion. "They'll put him away for a long time. He won't bother you, Lucille. Course, I guess you'll still have to call yourself Millard . . . or maybe whatever his right name is."

Ma hadn't thought that far, and she stared into space a minute. Then, with a lot of determination, she said, "No, I won't. I want to be Mrs. Parker James again. I'll divorce Joseph Millard."

Aunt Nelda gasped. "Lucille! You can't. The scandal it would cause. . . . No, it's impossible."

"It is not," Ma retorted. "I can and I will divorce him. It won't be any worse than being married to a bank robber who's in jail."

And Uncle Charlie said quietly, "I'll take you to talk to Judge Thomas in the morning, Lucille. He's handled some things for me, and I trust him."

Ma smiled her thanks, and Aunt Nelda just sniffed, as if she was really offended.

Summer began for me the next day, even though school had been out nearly a month already. Ma took over the running of the house. All of a sudden she had time to do it, what with no Joseph Millard to cater to. And yet losing Mr. Millard hadn't cost her one bit of energy. In fact, she was busier than ever, cooking and washing and taking care of Little Henry and Maggie. It left me with a lot of toe-stubbing time on my hands. Suddenly I was a kid again.

"Ellsbeth, what do you want to do today?"

Lavine and I sat on the front porch of our house early in the morning with a whole long, vacant day in front of us.

"Want to play cowboys and Indians?" B.J. was eager for company.

"No, B.J." There was summer boredom in my voice.

"How about swimming in the stock tank?"

"Can't. Ma'd have a fit."

B.J. looked at me as if I had the plague and went off to climb a tree.

"Lavine, what d'ya want to do?"

"Ellsbeth," she said in a funny, tiny voice. "I don't know what kinds of things you do in the summer here."

I looked at her for a minute. There was a whole world of things I had to teach her about, a world I'd put behind me when Pa died. Now I could rediscover it and share it with Lavine.

"Well, let's begin by hunting minnows in the creek, and then we can go out to. . . ." I stopped. I had been going to say we could go out and chunk rocks in the tank behind our old house, but I didn't want to go back there again. It was as though that house was behind me now, too; all its pleasant memories cancelled out by one bad time. The boarding-house was finally home.

"Out where?" Lavine asked.

"Over, I meant, over to Annabelle's and see if she'll give us some lemonade. But I gotta be home to help Ma with supper."

"I thought you didn't have to help anymore."

"Don't. But I want to. Come on, let's go. We've got a whole day!"

I looked up at that sky they call buttermilk and thought how wonderful summer is in East Texas!

Also available for 8-14 year old readers:

Maggie and a Horse Named Devildust
by Judy Alter

Maggie and the Search for Devildust
by Judy Alter

Maggie and Devildust Ridin' High
by Judy Alter

A Vampire Named Fred
by Bill Crider

How the Critters Created Texas
by F. E. Abernethy

The Reindeer's Shoe and Other Stories
by Karle Wilson Baker